WHO WILL SURVIVE?

IT'S GOING
TO BE A
KILLER
YEAR!

Is the senior class at Shadyside High doomed? That's
the prediction Trisha Conrad makes at her summer
party—and it looks as if she may be right. Spend a
year with the FEAR STREET seniors, as each month in
this new 12-book series brings horror after horror.
Will anyone reach graduation day alive?

Only R.L. Stine knows...

SHADYSIDE
HIGH
YEARBOOK

Mira Block

LIKES:
Going to clubs, guys in bands, sexy clothes

REMEMBERS:
The cemetery, senior camp-out, hanging out with Clarissa

HATES:
Waifs, talking on the phone, psychics

QUOTE:
"Don't hate me 'cause I'm beautiful."

Greta Bradley

LIKES:
Cheerleading, football players, all my cool friends

REMEMBERS:
The first time Ty asked me out, shopping at Chanel with Jade

HATES:
Ceramics, creepy houses, New Year's Eve

QUOTE:
"That boy is mine."

Trisha Conrad

LIKES:
Shopping in the mall my dad owns, giving fabulous parties, Gary Fresno

REMEMBERS:
The murder game, the senior table at Pete's Pizza

HATES:
Rich girl jokes, bad karma, overalls

QUOTE:
"What you don't know will hurt you."

Danielle Cortez

LIKES:
My ~~current~~ ~~boyfriend, cheering~~ the Tigers, dancing

REMEMBERS:
Trisha's ~~big~~ party, finally making varsity cheerleader

HATES:
The first day of ~~school~~, ~~pop quizzes~~, cold ~~cereals~~

QUOTE:
"Push 'em down, push 'em down, push 'em waaaay down! Go Tigers!"

REST IN PEACE

Clark Dickson

LIKES:
Debra Lake, poetry, painting

REMEMBERS:
Trisha's party, the first time I saw Debra

HATES:
Nicknames, dentists, garlic pizza, tans

QUOTE:
"Fangs for the memories."

Jennifer Fear

LIKES:
Basketball, antique jewelry, cool music

REMEMBERS:
The doom spell, senior cut day, hanging with Trisha and Josie

HATES:
The way people are afraid of the Fears, pierced eyebrows

QUOTE:
"There's nothing to fear but fear itself."

Jade Feldman

LIKES:
Cheerleading, expensive clothes, working out

REMEMBERS:
Ice cream and gab fests with Dana

HATES:
Cheerleading captains, ghosts, SAT prep courses

QUOTE:
"You get what you pay for."

Gary Fresno

LIKES:
Hanging out by the bleachers, art class, gym

REMEMBERS:
Cruisin' down Division Street with the guys, that special night with that special person (you know who you are...)

HATES:
My beat-up Civic, working after school everyday, cops

QUOTE:
"Don't judge a book by its cover."

Kenny Klein

LIKES:
Jade Feldman, chemistry, Latin, baseball

REMEMBERS:
The first time I beat Marla Newman in a debate, Junior Prom with Jade

HATES:
Nine-year-olds who like to torture camp counselors, cafeteria food

QUOTE:
"Look before you leap."

Debra Lake

LIKES:
Sensitive ~~guys, Clark's poems~~

REMEMBERS:
Basketball games, when Clark painted a portrait

HATES:
Possessive boyfriends and jealous girlfriends

QUOTE:
"I would do anything for you, but I won't do that."

REST IN PEACE

Stacy Malcolm

LIKES:
Sports, funky hats, shopping

REMEMBERS:
Running laps with Mary, stuffing our faces at Pete's, Mr. Morley and Rob

HATES:
Psycho killers, stealing boyfriends

QUOTE:
"College, here I come!"

Josh Maxwell

LIKES:
Debra Lake, Debra Lake, Debra Lake

REMEMBERS:
Hanging out at the old mill, senior camp-out, Coach's pep talks

HATES:
Funeral homes, driving my parents' car, tomato juice

QUOTE:
"Sometimes you don't realize the truth until it bites you right on the neck."

Josie Maxwell

LIKES:
Black clothes, black nail polish, black lipstick, photography

REMEMBERS:
Trisha's first senior party, the memorial wall

HATES:
Algebra, evil spirits (including Marla Newman), being compared to my stepbrother Josh

QUOTE:
"The past isn't always the past—sometimes it's the future."

Mickey Myers

LIKES:
Jammin' with the band, partying, hot girls

REMEMBERS:
Swimming in Fear Lake, the storm, my first gig at the Underground

HATES:
Dweebs, studying, girls who diet, station wagons

QUOTE:
"Shadyside High rules!"

Marla Newman

LIKES:
Writing, cool clothes, being a redhead

REMEMBERS:
Yearbook deadlines, competing with Kenny Klein, when Josie put a spell on me (ha ha)

HATES:
Girls who wear all black, guys with long hair, the dark arts

QUOTE:
"The power is divided when the circle is not round."

Mary O'Connor

LIKES:
Running, ripped jeans, hair spray

REMEMBERS:
Not being invited to Trisha's party, rat poison

HATES:
Social studies, rich girls, cliques

QUOTE:
"Just say no."

Dana Palmer

LIKES:
Boys, boys, boys, cheerleading, short skirts

REMEMBERS:
Senior camp-out with Mickey, Homecoming, the back seat

HATES:
Private cheerleading performances, fire batons, sharing clothes

QUOTE:
"The bad twin always wins!"

Deirdre Palmer

LIKES:
Mysterious guys, sharing clothes, old movies

REMEMBERS:
The cabin in the Fear Street woods, sleepovers at Jen's

HATES:
Being a "good girl," sweat socks

QUOTE:
"What you see isn't always what you get."

Will Reynolds

LIKES:
The Turner family, playing guitar, clubbing

REMEMBERS:
The first time Clarissa saw me without my dreads, our booth at Pete's

HATES:
Lite FM, the clinic, lilacs

QUOTE:
"I get knocked down, but I get up again…"

Ty Sullivan

LIKES:
Cheerleaders, waitresses, Fears, psychics, brains, football

REMEMBERS:
The graveyard with you know who, Kenny Klein's lucky shot

HATES:
Painting fences, Valentine's Day

QUOTE:
"The more the merrier."

Justin Thompson

LIKES:
Computers, that special person, the Beastie Boys, Barry White

REMEMBERS:
Don't want to remember anything about Shadyside

HATES:
Having my face shoved in the toilet, being chased by Ty and Gary

QUOTE:
"You're my everything."

Clarissa Turner

LIKES:
Art, music, talking on the phone

REMEMBERS:
Shopping with Debra, my first day back to school, eating pizza with Will

HATES:
Mira Block

QUOTE:
"Real friendship never dies."

Matty Winger

LIKES:
Computers, video games, Star Trek

REMEMBERS:
The murder game—good one Trisha

HATES:
People who can't take a joke, finding Clark's cape with Josh

QUOTE:
"Don't worry, be happy."

Phoebe Yamura

LIKES:
Cheerleading, gymnastics, big crowds

REMEMBERS:
That awesome game against Waynesbridge, senior trip, tailgate parties

HATES:
When people don't give it their all, liars, vans

QUOTE:
"Today is the first day of the rest of our lives."

The Gift

R.L. Stine
Seniors
a FEAR STREET series

episode six **The Gift**

A Parachute Press Book

A GOLD KEY PAPERBACK
Golden Books Publishing Company, Inc.
New York

Check out the new FEAR STREET® Website
http://www.fearstreet.com

A Gold Key Paperback Original

Golden Books Publishing Company, Inc.
888 Seventh Avenue
New York, NY 10106

ISBN: 0-307-24710-4

First Gold Key paperback printing December 1998

10 9 8 7 6 5 4 3 2

Photographer: Jimmy Levin

Printed in the U.S.A.

The Gift

J ennifer Fear trotted up the long, curving staircase of the Conrad mansion—eager to see her best friend, Trisha.

An evergreen garland, looped around the banister, filled the air with the scent of pine. Red and white poinsettias stood on the second-floor landing.

It was the day after Christmas.

Smiling to herself, Jennifer pulled off her lemon-yellow gloves and shoved them into her jacket pocket. She couldn't wait to show Trisha the incredible gift her parents had given her. She hurried down a wide hallway and burst into her friend's bedroom.

Blond and delicate-looking, Trisha sat on the bed with a bunch of pillows behind her, listening to music through a headset. She

1

smiled and pulled off the headset when she saw Jennifer.

"Hi! How was your Christmas?" Jennifer asked, unzipping her jacket.

Trisha shut off her Walkman and dropped the headset onto the bed. "Great," she replied. "I was just listening to one of my presents. You won't believe the stuff I got. Tons of it."

I can believe it, Jennifer thought. Trisha's father had built Shadyside's Division Street Mall and other big malls around the country.

The Conrads were super-rich. Their huge mansion sat at the top of River Ridge, overlooking the Conononka River. It had been in the family for more than a hundred years.

"Let me show you my favorite gift." Trisha scooted off the bed and crossed the room to her huge walk-in closet. She stepped inside and came right back out a few seconds later wearing a black leather jacket.

"Whoa—that's awesome!" Jennifer exclaimed. She walked over and touched the leather. "It's so soft. It almost feels like velvet."

"I know. It's—" Trisha broke off. "Hey. What's that around your neck?"

"It's *my* favorite present." Jennifer took off her own jacket and tossed it onto the bed.

She shook back her long brown hair and turned around to reveal the necklace her parents had given her the day before.

Trisha sucked in her breath in admiration.

The chain was made of intricate gold links. A dark red stone hung from the chain, and nestled at the base of Jennifer's throat.

The stone was set in heavy gold, almost half an inch across.

"It's gorgeous!" Trisha exclaimed.

"Thanks. I was totally amazed when I opened it," Jennifer told her. "I knew it was jewelry because of the box, but no way did I expect something like this!"

Trisha fingered the gold chain and peered at the red stone. "Is it a ruby?"

Jennifer shook her head. "It's a garnet. Dad had it checked out."

"What do you mean? Didn't the jewelry store know?"

"He didn't get it at a jewelry store," Jennifer replied. "He said he found it in a junk shop in the Old Village." She turned the garnet over. "Look."

Inscribed on the heavy gold backing was a woman's name.

Dominique Fear.

Trisha's eyebrows rose in surprise. "You mean this necklace belongs in your family? And you're *wearing* it? I thought you hated *any*thing to do with the name Fear."

Jennifer gave an embarrassed laugh. "I did, until I saw this necklace," she admitted.

"It's so cool, I couldn't resist it. Dad says it's from the nineteenth century."

"So who was Dominique?" Trisha asked.

Jennifer shrugged. "My dad might know," she said. "He has tons of old Fear papers and books. But I don't care about that stuff. I just like the necklace."

The phone rang. Trisha hung her leather jacket on a bedpost and answered it. "It's Gary," she mouthed to Jennifer.

While Trisha talked to her boyfriend, Gary Fresno, Jennifer sat down on the cushioned window seat at the front of the room.

Staring out over the cliff toward the Conononka River, she thought about her ancestors.

The Fears.

They had come to Shadyside sometime in the 1800s. And the town's people thought the Fears were evil. Jennifer wasn't sure why.

Something to do with an unexplained death.

A mysterious fire.

A supernatural force, reaching out from the grave to kill.

Yeah, right. Jennifer shook her head. Like that could really happen.

She couldn't believe people actually bought into that evil Fear stuff.

Even today almost everyone in town knew

at least one Fear story. And the kids at school didn't need an excuse to tease her about being a Fear.

Jennifer grew up hating her last name.

Unfortunately, her father was totally obsessed with his ancestry. They even lived across from the creepy burnt-out Fear mansion on Fear Street. Jennifer hated seeing it every day.

She wasn't crazy about her own house, either. It was a Fear house, too. Huge and gloomy, with tall pine trees that blocked the sunlight.

But her father loved it.

Over the years he scoured the town for anything he could find that belonged to the family. He filled the downstairs library with every Fear letter and paper that he could get his hands on. And ancient books—books that gave instructions on how to cast evil spells.

A few months ago Jennifer, Deirdre Palmer, and Josie Maxwell even tried to perform one of those spells.

A doom spell.

On Josie's math teacher, Mr. Torkelson.

He then died in a horrible accident.

But that was just a coincidence, Jennifer thought.

Of course, Dad found this necklace, too, Jennifer reminded herself. At least all that collecting wasn't a *total* waste.

Trisha hung up and joined Jennifer on the window seat. "Gary wanted to go out tonight, but my parents are having guests and I have to be here," she reported. "So. Is everything ready for your New Year's Eve party?"

"Just about," Jennifer replied. "I'm really excited—this is the first New Year's Eve party I've ever given."

"Are you going to use the ballroom?"

"No way. I want it to be a *normal* party," Jennifer told her. "Nobody else in town has a ballroom, not even you. Besides, it's too far away from the kitchen. The living room will be perfect. Anyway, the party is going to be great. *And* you-know-who is going to be there!"

"Ty, you mean," Trisha replied.

"Who else?" Jennifer laughed.

Ty Sullivan moved to Shadyside over the summer, next door to Jennifer's house on Fear Street. He was tall and blond, and on the football team.

All the girls wanted to go out with Ty.

Jennifer thought he'd never notice her, but he finally did. They'd been seeing each other for weeks. And they were going out again that night.

"I still can't believe Ty picked me to be with," Jennifer declared.

A small frown appeared on Trisha's face.

6

"What?" Jennifer asked. "Don't you think it's great that I'm going out with him?"

"Sure I do." Trisha bit her lip. "But . . . well, I just don't think you should be *too* crazy about him."

"What's *that* supposed to mean?" Jennifer asked.

"Well . . ." Trisha hesitated. "He has this habit of seeing lots of girls. You know, at the same time."

Jennifer felt her cheeks flush. I know all about Ty, she thought, fingering the heavy garnet at her throat. He's cheated on a lot of girls at Shadyside High. But it's different with us. Ty says he really cares about me. Why did Trisha have to bring up all his old girlfriends?

"Jen, I'm sorry," Trisha told her. "Ty's obviously crazy about you. Just you. Forget what I said. It was stupid."

"That's okay." Jennifer shook off the feeling of irritation. Trisha is my friend, that's all, she thought. She doesn't want me to get hurt.

Trisha pointed to the necklace. "I'm dying to try that on. Could I?"

"Sure . . . if I can try on your new jacket," Jennifer added.

Trisha laughed. "Deal."

Jennifer stood up. Trisha unhooked the necklace and slipped it around her own

7

throat. Jennifer clasped it for her, then crossed the room and took the leather jacket from the bedpost.

Jennifer pulled on the jacket and zipped it up. "How do I look?" she asked.

Trisha didn't reply.

Her face went pale. Her brown eyes stared blankly at Jennifer, as if she were a stranger.

"Trisha?" Jennifer hurried to her friend's side. "What is it? What's wrong?"

Trisha continued to stare, not moving. Not blinking.

She's having a vision, Jennifer thought. Another psychic flash.

Trisha has been having visions since she was a little girl. She could see things—things that would happen in the future.

Like the vision she had about the senior class, Jennifer thought with a shiver. It was the worst flash Trisha ever had.

She saw the entire senior class rotting in their graves.

And since school opened in September, four people had died.

Mr. Torkelson, Danielle Cortez, Ms. Sanders, Debra Lake . . .

And two transfer students had mysteriously disappeared at the start of the school year. Anita Black and Jon something.

"Trisha!" Jennifer began to shake her friend's shoulder. "Please, snap out of it."

Trisha stared for a few seconds longer. Finally her eyes focused.

"What was it?" Jennifer demanded. "What did you see?"

Trisha took a deep, shaky breath. "I saw her die," she declared in a low voice. "They put a noose around her neck and hanged her!"

Chapter TWO

Trisha's eyes darkened with horror. "I saw her die!" she repeated. "I saw it happen. I could almost feel it!"

An icy chill crept up Jennifer's back. "Another senior? Who was she?"

"I don't know. I mean, I don't think it was anyone in our class," Trisha replied. "She was young. Very pretty, with dark hair. She died a long time ago."

"How do you know that?" Jennifer asked.

"Her dress was really old-fashioned. It had a long skirt and lace around the neck." Trisha paused, gazing into the distance. "Her boots buttoned up the side. And she wore her hair all piled up on her head. It came loose when they put the rope on."

Jennifer shuddered. I really don't want

to hear this, she thought.

"It was awful," Trisha continued. "She was terrified. But she was furious, too. I felt *that* more than anything. She was totally full of anger. And hate."

"Look, try to forget about it," Jennifer suggested. "You said it happened a long time ago. You can't do anything about it."

"I know," Trisha murmured. "But the feeling was so strong." She glanced down at the necklace and turned the garnet over. "Dominique Fear. This was hers. Maybe that's who I saw."

"Maybe," Jennifer said. She didn't want to talk about it.

"I wonder why she was hanged," Trisha went on. "What do you think she did?"

Jennifer shrugged a little impatiently. "The Fear family history is my father's thing, not mine. You of all people should know that."

Trisha reached back and unclasped the necklace. "Here," she said, holding it out. "It's beautiful, but it creeps me out a little."

Jennifer rolled her eyes. She couldn't believe that Trisha was freaking out like this. "Hey, it's only a necklace." She slid out of the jacket and gave it to Trisha. "It's not like it's evil or anything."

"Ty! This is the cemetery!" Jennifer

exclaimed later that night. "Why did you turn the car in here?"

Ty glanced at her. His eyes glittered. "You'll see," he said, smiling.

He continued to steer his black Celica over the frozen, bumpy ruts of an old dirt lane that cut through the Fear Street Cemetery.

Jennifer gazed out the window. Frost covered the headstones. Old and tilted, they seemed to be sinking down into the earth.

Sinking toward the dead.

Jennifer shivered and glanced at Ty. She admired his square jaw, full lips and strong hands. She even liked the small gold ring that glinted from his eyebrow.

He's so hot, she thought. And I had such a great time tonight. A movie. Some pizza. But now—the cemetery?

Ty pulled the car to a stop and slipped a CD into the slot. As the music started, he turned sideways in his seat to face Jennifer. "Scared?" he asked.

"Well . . . this place is kind of creepy," she replied.

Ty stretched out his arm. "Come here," he said. "I won't let anything happen to you."

Jennifer scooted over. Ty put both arms around her and kissed her, hard.

Jennifer kissed him back. Her heart pounded like crazy.

"Still scared?" he murmured, his lips against her cheek.

"Not so much." Jennifer pulled back and gazed into his eyes. "So that's the trick, huh? You bring girls here and they get scared. Then they forget all about it the minute they start making out with you."

"You got it. It works every time." Ty traced a finger around her lips, then kissed her again.

Jennifer closed her eyes. He's right, she thought. I don't mind being in a cemetery with him. I don't mind being anywhere as long as I'm with Ty.

Ty kissed her harder. Then his lips slid across her cheek to her neck.

With a sigh, Jennifer tilted her head back. His lips moved softly down the side of her neck toward her throat.

Jennifer quivered at the touch.

With a sudden gasp, Ty jerked away. "Hey!"

Jennifer opened her eyes, startled. "What's wrong?"

Ty didn't answer. He touched his chin, then winced and pulled his hand away.

A dark smear remained on his chin.

Something wet trickled down Jennifer's neck. She touched it and peered at her wet fingertips.

"It's blood!" she cried.

Chapter Three

"**B**lood? What did you do to me?" Ty demanded angrily.

"I didn't do anything!" she cried. "It's on me, too. I don't know where it came from."

Jennifer felt her neck again. It didn't hurt at all. "I'm not cut or anything," she said. She felt her neck. "I don't get it. Where did the . . . ohhhhhh!"

"Oh, *what*?" Ty asked.

"My necklace." Jennifer reached up and turned on the dome light. "I guess it scraped you when you were kissing my neck."

She lightly brushed her hand across the heavy pendant. Blood smeared onto her fingertips. "See?" She showed Ty her hand. "It's kind of sharp."

"Yeah." Ty leaned his head back and puffed out a breath.

"Here." Jennifer pulled a couple of linty tissues from her bag and handed him one. She used the other one to wipe her neck and fingers, then glanced around for a place to put the tissue.

"Give me that." Ty opened the car window and tossed the balled-up tissues onto the frozen ground.

"Brr!" Jennifer shivered as a gust of icy wind blew into the car. "Roll it up, quick."

Ty closed the window, clicked the dome light off, and started the car.

As he began driving out of the cemetery, Jennifer scooted closer to him. "I really had fun tonight," she murmured.

"Yeah. Good." Ty pulled onto Fear Street.

"Do you want to do something tomorrow?" she asked. "I'm going to the library in the morning."

"Going to the library's not exactly my idea of a good time," he told her.

Jennifer laughed. "I meant afterward," she explained. "I still have some stuff to get for New Year's Eve. We could meet at the library and go to the mall. I was going to go for some pizza with Trisha tomorrow, but she won't mind if I don't. Maybe I'll skip basketball practice tomorrow, too."

He shook his head. "The mall drives me

nuts during the holidays. I feel like I'm in a mosh pit."

"Oh. Well, we could do something else. What about ice skating?" Jennifer suggested.

Ty pulled the car to a stop in front of Jennifer's house. They climbed out of their seats and walked up the icy path to the front door in silence.

"I haven't gone skating yet, have you?" Jennifer asked when they reached the porch.

"Uh, no," Ty replied. He shoved his hands in his jacket pockets, and glanced over his shoulder.

"So, do you want to do that?" Jennifer asked. "I'll bring my skates to the library and we can go from there. But if you don't want to, we could see another movie. Or—"

"Whoa, hang on a sec," Ty interrupted.

Jennifer paused. "Sure. What is it?"

He turned his head and gazed toward his car again.

"Ty? What's the matter?" she asked.

He kept staring at his car, not looking at her. "Listen. I think maybe we should slow down a little."

Jennifer's heart took a plunge. "What do you mean?" she asked. Stupid question, she thought. I know what he means. I know exactly what's coming.

Ty shrugged. "I just think we shouldn't see each other so much, that's all."

Jennifer didn't bother to ask why. I know why, she thought. Trisha warned me about this. And I knew it all along. I just didn't want to believe it. "It's true, isn't it?" she said. "You're seeing someone else."

"Well . . ." Ty glanced down at his shoes for a moment, then gazed back at Jennifer. "Yeah," he admitted. "I am. I mean, we never said we wouldn't go out with other people."

"I know." A lump rose in Jennifer's throat. She swallowed hard. "But I thought you really cared about me," she managed to choke out. "You said—"

"I do," Ty interrupted her.

Jennifer smiled bitterly. "Yeah, right. That's why you're dumping me."

"No, I do care," Ty insisted. "But I like to have fun, okay? You're so serious."

"What are you talking about? I like to have fun, too!" Jennifer exclaimed.

"Look, forget it, okay?" he declared impatiently. "Let's just not see each other. It'll be better that way."

Jennifer's eyes started to fill with tears. She quickly turned away. She didn't get it. Why was he doing this? She gazed at Ty. "But I . . ." Her bottom lip began to quiver.

Don't beg, she told herself. No matter what, don't get hysterical.

And don't let him see you cry!

Jennifer threw open the front door.

Slammed it shut. And raced up the stairs to her room.

Cold. So cold.

She clutched her arms and shivered as she walked through the night. She should have worn her woolen cape, she told herself.

And her thin silk slippers gave no protection from the frozen, frosted ground. Her feet ached from the cold.

The wind gusted, blowing her long skirt against her legs. Her hair whipped around her head. She peeled a strand from her eyes and gazed up.

Wispy, fingerlike clouds blew across the black sky. The moon was an icy silver disk.

She shivered again, violently.

But I must go on, she thought. Night is the only safe time.

The only time no one will see me.

No one will know.

She picked up her skirt and continued her journey. The wind tore the tears from her eyes. It slammed against her, making her stagger. Her hands and feet grew numb.

She kept walking.

She could not let the wind and the cold stop her.

Nothing must stop her.

Slowly she made her way along the frozen path and across the crackling, icy grass. By the time she reached her destination, the cold seemed to be coming from inside her.

But she was there at last.

At his house!

The sight of it warmed her. Started a fire deep inside. The heat raced through her veins. Her heart began to pound.

He doesn't know I am here, she thought. He does not care, but *I* do.

I do.

The house stood in front of her, a dark, hulking shape. Completely dark.

No.

A single light burned in an upstairs window.

Is it *his* light?

It must be. It has to be.

She took a few steps closer. She cupped her hands around her eyes and gazed up.

Her scream tore through the night like the shriek of the wind.

Chapter Four

Jennifer slowly opened her eyes.

Far above her head, a cloud blew by.

The moon shined down.

"I'm dreaming," she murmured. She closed her eyes and rolled to her side.

Something crackled underneath her. Something cold and wet.

What *is* that?

Jennifer propped herself on one elbow and stared down at her flannel sheets.

Except she didn't see her sheets. She saw grass. Frozen grass.

Jennifer's mind still felt fuzzy. As she tried to figure out what was going on, an icy wind gusted.

She gasped. Wide awake now, she shook with cold. And fear.

I'm not dreaming, she realized. I'm not even in bed.

I'm outside, lying on the ground.

What happened? How did I get here? The last thing Jennifer remembered was crying in her room. Crying after Ty dumped her.

The wind blew again.

Shivering, Jennifer braced herself on her hands and knees and tried to stand.

But something stopped her. Something wrapped around her, and she fell onto the frozen grass.

Jennifer rolled over and sat, staring at the white material twisted around her legs. "My nightgown?"

Jennifer gasped. I guess I was sleepwalking, she thought. Why else would I be outside in my nightgown in the middle of the night?

Her eyes darted frantically across the dark landscape. The wind whistled past her ears. She shivered again.

Where am I? she wondered.

Another cloud blocked the moon. She couldn't see anything but a bunch of black, hulking shapes.

Where *am* I?

With a whimper, she untangled the gown and stumbled to her feet. The gown was frozen at the hem and wet on the back. Melted frost and mud soaked through the bottoms of her slippers.

Shaking with cold, she clutched her arms and glanced around.

The cloud blew by.

A cold, silver light fell across everything. Leafless trees. A tall hedge with a dirt path cutting through it. A wide yard of brittle grass.

The back of a house.

Jennifer peered at it. Is it mine?

No.

It's . . . Ty's house!

I'm in Ty's backyard!

Why did I come here?

A cry of confusion and fear rose in her throat. Clapping a hand over her mouth, she turned and ran.

Jennifer entered the Shadyside library the next day and hurried past the checkout desk into the main room.

Rows of computers lined a wall. Trisha sat at one of them, peering intently at the screen. Jennifer knew Trisha was on the Internet, researching for her college application essay. Trisha wanted to go to Duke University. Her application was due the week after winter break. Jennifer's application for the University of Wisconsin was due the same week.

Just about everybody's applications were due that week.

Jennifer and Trisha both wanted to get their essays over with as fast as possible. They agreed to work together for a while, then go get some pizza.

Jennifer sighed. I guess I'll go to basketball practice later, too.

Of course, Jennifer *thought* she might be seeing Ty this afternoon.

That was before last night, though. Before he broke up with her.

Tears started to prickle at Jennifer's eyes, but she blinked them back. She didn't want to think about that now. She still felt awful, but something else was bothering her.

The sleepwalking.

Why did I do that? she wondered.

Did I want to see Ty or something? I know I fell asleep thinking about him. Feeling so rotten because he dumped me.

Maybe I dreamed so hard about wanting to change things that I actually got up and went to talk to him.

It made sense, but Jennifer couldn't help feeling frightened about it.

It's as if I didn't have any control, she thought.

Someone brushed past her, jostling her backpack. She hitched it up on her shoulder and crossed the carpeted room, heading for the computer row.

Trisha glanced up as she approached. "Hi.

There's tons of stuff on college applications."

"Great." Jennifer dropped her backpack and stuffed her gloves into her jacket pocket. She fumbled with the zipper. Her hand shook.

"What's wrong?" Trisha asked. "You're all pale. Are you sick?"

"Uh . . . no." Jennifer finally got the zipper undone. She pulled off her jacket and slid another chair over.

As she sat down, she nervously touched the garnet at her throat.

Her hand still shook.

"Jen, what's the matter with you?" Trisha repeated.

Jennifer glanced around. She didn't want anyone to hear what she had to say.

Kenny Klein was across the room at a long table, his head bent over a bunch of papers.

Deirdre Palmer stood at the checkout desk with a pile of books in her arms.

Deirdre caught Jennifer's eye and waved, but she didn't get out of line.

A couple of other seniors were in the room, but they were too far away to hear.

Jennifer leaned close to Trisha. "Something really scary happened last night," she murmured quietly. "I walked in my sleep."

Trisha's eyes widened. "Really?"

Jennifer nodded. "I woke up lying on the ground. My nightgown was all muddy and I was practically freezing to death."

"That's weird," Trisha declared.

"I know. I haven't done that since I was in kindergarten." Jennifer shuddered. "It really scared me."

"Well, but you're okay, right?" Trisha asked.

"Yes, but . . ." Jennifer leaned closer and lowered her voice to a whisper. "Trisha, when I woke up I was in—"

Jennifer broke off as she heard someone approach.

Phoebe Yamura, head of the cheerleading squad, stopped next to Jennifer's chair. "Did you guys hear about Ty Sullivan?" she asked seriously.

Jennifer stiffened. A wave of unease rippled up her spine.

"What about him?" Trisha asked.

"He was attacked last night," Phoebe declared. "In his own backyard!"

Chapter Five

Jennifer tried to stifle a gasp of horror.

Ty! Attacked in his yard last night, she thought. Where I was sleepwalking!

"Was he . . . killed?" she choked out.

Phoebe shook her head. "No. But he's got a major gash on his head. I saw him this morning. He's all bandaged up."

"That's awful!" Trisha cried. "Who did it?"

Phoebe shrugged. "Ty doesn't know. He didn't even see it coming." She glanced over Jennifer's shoulder. "I have to tell Deirdre."

Phoebe dashed across the room toward the book checkout area.

Jennifer stared after her, shocked and frightened. What happened last night? she wondered helplessly. Did I witness the attack or something?

26

"Jen!" Trisha prodded Jennifer's arm. "You were supposed to go out with Ty last night, right? Did you see him?"

Jennifer nodded.

"Well? What happened?"

"He . . ." Jennifer hesitated. She didn't want to tell. It was humiliating. But Trisha was her best friend. "We broke up," she confessed.

"What? You broke up? Why?" Trisha demanded in complete surprise.

"It's just like you said, Trish," Jennifer admitted. "He was going out with another girl the same time as me. At first, he just wanted to stop seeing me so much. But then he said I'm too serious and we should stop going out altogether."

"I'm really sorry, Jen," Trisha murmured sympathetically. "You must feel awful."

"Yeah, I do. I went to bed feeling totally rotten. And angry, too. I couldn't believe he dumped me like that." Jennifer bit her lip anxiously. "And Trisha . . . there's something else."

"Tell me," Trisha demanded.

Jennifer took a deep breath. "When I walked in my sleep, I went to Ty's house. That's where I was when I woke up—lying on the ground in his backyard."

"You're kidding!" Trisha cried.

Jennifer shook her head. "I don't know why I went there. And now he's been attacked!"

"Shhh." Trisha glanced around. "There are too many people here," she declared. "Come on. Let's find someplace else to talk."

Trisha rose and walked through the shelves of books to a small deserted area by a fire exit.

Jennifer followed.

"Tell me everything," Trisha demanded quietly, after checking to make sure no one was around.

Jennifer described the night before. Going to a movie and getting something to eat with Ty. Making out in the cemetery. "I thought everything was going great," she said. "Then he cut himself and after that—"

"What?" Trisha interrupted. "Phoebe said he got cut in his yard."

"No. Well, I guess he did, but that's not what I was talking about," Jennifer told her. "This was *before*, when we were sitting in his car at the cemetery. And it wasn't like this major cut. It was just a stupid little scratch on his chin."

"How did it happen?"

"Ty was kissing me." A lump rose in Jennifer's throat and she swallowed hard. "He was kissing my neck and my necklace scratched him somehow."

Trisha reached out and fingered Jennifer's pendant. She frowned slightly, then raised her eyes and stared at Jennifer.

"Anyway, we left the cemetery after that," Jennifer continued. "And I started talking about doing stuff today. Going ice skating or seeing another movie or something. That's when Ty said we should slow down. Then he decided it was totally over."

Trisha kept staring at Jennifer.

No. Not *at* me, Jennifer realized. *Through* me. She's seeing something else.

She's having another vision.

Trisha's brown eyes grew almost black as the pupils expanded. Her face went pale, and her jaw muscles quivered as she clenched her teeth.

I've never seen her like this before, Jennifer thought. She looks kind of angry. Bitter.

"Trisha!" Jennifer whispered. She gave her friend's arm a shake. "Earth to Trisha!"

Trisha continued staring a few seconds longer. Finally her face relaxed and her eyes focused on Jennifer.

"You had another vision, didn't you?" Jennifer asked. "What did you see?"

"Um . . . nothing. It was nothing," Trisha replied quickly. "Listen, I just remembered— I have to go over to my grandmother's. She wants to see me before she goes to France. Let's forget about the party supplies for now, okay?"

"No, it's not okay!" Jennifer cried. "Not

until you tell me what you saw! The expression on your face—it scared me, Trisha!"

Trisha bit her lip.

"Please," Jennifer urged.

"Okay," Trisha agreed reluctantly. "I had a flash of the attack on Ty. It was kind of blurry, and I don't know exactly what happened, but . . . it was like I was in the attacker's head. Like I was looking out through her eyes."

"*Her* eyes?" Jennifer felt another ripple of unease. She touched the cold garnet at her throat. "Are you saying . . ."

"I'm not saying anything!" Trisha interrupted. "Jen, I'll meet you later at Pete's. I have to go!"

"But, Trisha . . ." Jennifer grabbed her arm.

Trisha glanced at Jennifer's hand on her arm. Then she glared into Jennifer's eyes and sneered. "Don't try to stop me," she muttered through her teeth. "Let *go* of my arm."

Shocked, Jennifer unclasped Trisha's arm and anxiously fingered the garnet around her neck.

Without a word Trisha hurried away.

Jennifer stared after Trisha, a little shaken and worried.

Something's wrong, she finally decided. Something's *very* wrong.

Chapter Six

Jennifer bit into a slice of pizza and glanced quickly at Trisha from under her eyelashes.

Her friend sat across from her in the booth at Pete's Pizza, staring around the crowded restaurant.

Jennifer followed her gaze. She noticed Greta Bradley, one of the cheerleaders, sitting with Jade Feldman and Kenny Klein.

But Trisha wasn't looking at them. She didn't seem to be looking at anyone.

What is on her mind? Jennifer wondered. What did she see in her vision?

Feeling Jennifer's eyes on her, Trisha turned back. "Sorry I had to run out on you," she murmured.

"That's okay." Except she didn't really

31

have to go, Jennifer thought. She wanted to get away. Whatever she saw and felt in that vision really upset her. That's why she freaked out in the library. That's why she still looks worried.

Jennifer had decided not to say anything about it. Trisha obviously didn't want to.

And neither do I, she thought. That bitter, angry expression on Trisha's face was creepy. I'd rather forget it.

Jennifer popped a piece of cheese into her mouth and picked up her Coke.

Trisha suddenly gasped. "Jennifer! Look!"

Jennifer followed Trisha's gaze again.

Ty had just entered the restaurant.

Jennifer's heart felt as if it had stopped.

A thick gauze bandage covered the left side of Ty's forehead. Some kind of thread peeked out from the edges.

Stitches, Jennifer realized with a jolt. Whoever attacked Ty cut him so badly he needed stitches!

Her hands began to shake. She set her Coke down. "I have to talk to him."

Jennifer started to slide out of the booth, but Trisha reached across the table and grabbed her arm. "No, wait!"

"I just . . ." Jennifer glanced at Ty again.

Even across the restaurant, she could see that sexy, admiring gleam in his eyes.

But it wasn't for her.

It was for Greta Bradley, dashing through the crowded restaurant to Ty's side.

Jennifer wanted to run somewhere. Hide and never come out.

But she couldn't move. She stood frozen, watching the tall blond cheerleader wrap her arm around Ty's waist. Seeing him lean close and kiss her on the lips.

So Greta's the one he's been seeing, Jennifer thought. Since when did Greta Bradley get to be so much *fun*? she wondered bitterly. Greta's practically made of ice.

Jennifer shook her head. It doesn't matter whether Greta is fun. Ty just wanted to move on, that's all.

As Ty and Greta joined Kenny and Jade at their table, Jennifer slowly sank back into the booth. Her knees felt wobbly and her eyes filled with tears.

A couple of tears spilled over. She swiped them away and squeezed her eyes shut.

Get a grip, she told herself. Don't fall apart now, not in the middle of Pete's. Not when Ty might see you!

She took a deep, shaky breath. Then another.

When she was sure she wouldn't cry, she opened her eyes.

Trisha was staring at Greta's table. Her lips were pressed together in a thin, angry line. "How could he do this?" she muttered though clenched teeth. "How could he?"

Jennifer flinched at the sound of Trisha's voice. It was so different. Deeper, somehow. Thick and harsh, as if the very words were choking her.

"How could he do this?" Trisha repeated.

"Let's not talk about it, not here," Jennifer told her quickly. "Let's just get out—"

"He's a total jerk!" Trisha interrupted. Her voice rose and her eyes flashed with anger.

"Shhh, Trisha, don't yell," Jennifer pleaded.

"Why not?" Trisha demanded, her voice rising even more. "I'm furious. Aren't you?"

Jennifer stared at her friend's angry face. I have to calm her down, she told herself. I can't let her freak out in the middle of Pete's.

"Look, you *did* warn me about Ty," Jennifer said, keeping her voice as steady and quiet as possible. "He was probably seeing Greta while he was seeing me."

Trisha glared at her. "Don't you even *care*?" she asked. Then she raised her voice again. "Aren't you even *angry?*"

"I—I . . ." Jennifer didn't know what to say. Some of the other kids in the restaurant started staring.

"I can't believe this!" Trisha went on.

Jennifer was getting embarrassed. Trisha was acting totally weird. And a little scary.

"I'm a little upset, but it's no big deal, Trisha," Jennifer lied, trying to calm her friend down. "Like you said, Ty is a jerk. I really don't care. I swear."

"You want to come over to my house for dinner?" Stacy Malcolm asked as Jennifer drove her home after basketball practice that evening.

Jennifer shook her head no. "Thanks, but it's kind of been a rough day."

"Tell me about it," Stacy replied. "I think everyone's been stressing over college applications."

"Yeah," Jennifer said as she gazed through the windshield, not really paying attention to the conversation. She could not stop thinking about Ty. About how he was attacked the night before. And how she had woken up in his backyard.

Jennifer winced as she remembered the bloody bandage on Ty's forehead.

"By the way," Stacy said, breaking Jennifer's thoughts. "What was up with Trisha in Pete's today? I mean, she totally made a scene. What was that all about?"

Jennifer wasn't really sure why Trisha had acted so weird. She was even a little worried about her. Jennifer had never seen Trisha so furious before.

She cleared her throat and glanced at

Stacy. "I don't know. I guess she was angry . . . because Ty broke up with me." Tears began to sting her eyes, and Jennifer fought to hold them back.

"Oh, Jen! That's terrible." Stacy placed her hand on Jennifer's shoulder. "Are you okay?"

"Yeah," Jennifer replied, trying to smile a little.

She pulled in front of Stacy's house, and Stacy climbed out of her seat.

"I'll talk to you later," Stacy said. "And Jen . . . try not to think about Ty. Trisha's right. He's a total jerk."

Jennifer waved and pulled away from the curb.

A thick fog was rolling in, and she turned the headlights to bright. They barely cut through the dense, swirling moisture.

Jennifer flipped on the defroster and pulled onto Park Drive. Her mind immediately returned to Ty.

That horrible bandage on his head. Those ugly stitches. What happened last night?

Who attacked him? Trisha probably thinks *I* did it, Jennifer told herself. She won't say so, but I know it's true. In that vision she was inside the attacker's head.

"I saw it through *her* eyes," Trisha had said.

Who else could she have been talking about but me? Jennifer wondered. Nobody else was in Ty's yard last night.

Jennifer shivered. The car had warmed up, but she still felt cold. It's not the weather, she thought as she turned onto Fear Street. It's me.

I don't understand what is going on! I walked in my sleep, to Ty's yard. But I couldn't have attacked him, could I? I've never done anything to hurt anyone, ever.

A shadowy figure suddenly appeared in front of her car.

A man.

Close.

So close.

"No!" Jennifer screamed. She whipped the wheel to the right. The car skidded on a patch of ice, and it sailed forward.

Jennifer pumped the brakes.

Too late.

The figure was inches away, looming up out of the thick, swirling fog.

"I can't stop!" Jennifer cried.

Chapter Seven

"**N**o!" Jennifer screamed again.

The car sped forward. Jennifer cringed, helplessly waiting for that horrible thud against the front bumper.

Nothing happened.

The car continued to glide along the ice.

Jennifer quickly glanced in the rearview mirror. She couldn't see anything through the fog.

Did I hit him? she wondered in a panic.

The car suddenly fishtailed and began to swing around in a wide arc. Jennifer gripped the wheel tightly, desperately trying not to lose control.

She pumped the brakes again.

The tires caught. The car began to slow. She let out a cry of relief.

I'm off the ice.

The car screeched to a stop, facing in the direction she came from. Jennifer shoved the gear stick into park and threw the door open, almost falling out onto the cold black street.

She caught her balance and gazed down the road.

Through the rolling fog, she saw the figure climbing to its feet near the curb.

"Are you okay?" she shouted, beginning to run. "Did I hit you?"

She heard a muffled reply, but she couldn't make the words out. Please let him be okay, she prayed.

"I'm sorry!" she cried. "The fog's so thick I didn't see you until the last second. Did I hit you? Are you all right?"

The figure straightened up and stared at her.

Jennifer gasped.

It was Ty.

Her headlights pierced the fog just enough for her to see his face. His angry, frightened eyes. The blood trickling from the bandage on his forehead.

"You're bleeding," she told him. "One of your stitches must have come loose when you jumped."

"When you almost ran me down, you mean," Ty declared angrily. "I was just trying to get someone to stop. My car broke down. What were you trying to do—kill me?"

"What? No! I'm sorry!" Jennifer told him. "I didn't see—"

"Just stay away from me!" Ty shouted, cutting her off. "Do you hear? Stay *away* from me!"

Fog drifted and writhed along the ground like smoke.

But overhead, the moon was out. A misty moon, with clouds scudding across its face. Still, its light was strong enough to guide her along the path.

She moved quickly, her feet in warm calfskin boots. No slippers tonight. She had dressed for the weather, with gloves and a long woolen muffler around her neck.

She patted her pocket. The small box still nestled there. Dry and safe.

Tonight I am prepared, she thought.

And I will do what I must do.

Nothing will stop me.

The fog began to thin as she reached her destination. Good. She would be able to see more clearly. But the fog provided cover, too.

She had to be quick before it vanished and exposed her.

She reached into her pocket and drew out the box. It slipped and fell to the ground. She tried to pick it up, but the thick gloves made her hands clumsy.

She quickly pulled the gloves off. The cold, damp air chilled her fingers almost immediately. She blew on them, then grasped the box.

Carefully she slid it open. The wind gusted. Her hands grew colder, began to shake. She struggled to steady them.

Be quick! she told herself. Do what you must do!

She took a deep breath and glanced down.

She held the box in her left hand.

And in her right hand, the match.

Jennifer bolted up, her heart thumping hard against her chest.

Where am I? I feel so cold.

Am I outside again?

She blinked and glanced all around, nervously touching the garnet at her throat.

Her dresser stood against one wall. A chair stood against another, with a bunch of clothes draped over its back. Her closet door was half-open, as usual.

I'm in my room, she thought with relief. In bed. I was only dreaming.

Jennifer stiffened. But I was dreaming about being in Ty's backyard.

Was it a dream? Or did I sleepwalk again?

She kicked the quilt down and checked her nightgown. No mud this time.

She reached over the side of the bed and felt for her slippers. Dry.

Yes. Just a dream.

Jennifer shivered, even though the room was warm. She pulled the quilt up to her neck.

In her dream she was walking through the night again. Walking along the path between her house and Ty's.

She could still see the misty moon and the fog swirling along the ground.

She could still feel the wind on her face and hands.

In her dream her hands were cold.

So cold!

She walked into Ty's yard and stopped. Then she . . . what? What happened then?

Jennifer shook her head. She couldn't remember anymore.

Her heart pounded faster. What happened after I went to Ty's yard? What?

Jennifer nervously twisted her hair through her fingers. It doesn't matter that you can't remember, she told herself. It was just a dream. It's not like you want to hurt Ty. It's not like you had anything to do with him being attacked.

Then Jennifer glanced at her bedside

clock. Almost ten in the morning.

Oh, no! She had to hurry. She was supposed to pick Trisha up at ten so they could go to the mall and buy noisemakers and confetti for the New Year's Eve party.

Jennifer threw the quilt back again. She raised the shade on her window, then hurried into the bathroom. She took a quick shower and dried her hair for a minute.

Back in the bedroom she pulled on her jeans and a dark blue turtleneck and tied her still-damp hair into a ponytail.

She ran downstairs to the kitchen, carrying her sneakers. She grabbed an apple and took a couple of bites, then put on her shoes and unhooked her jacket from the coat rack by the door.

Her car keys. Where were they? Jennifer patted her jacket pockets. The keys jingled. She'd stuffed her gloves in the other pocket. She pulled them out.

One of them, anyway. One lemon-yellow glove with tiny white snowflakes knitted into it.

What happened to the other one?

Jennifer scanned the floor and checked the inside pocket of her jacket. No stray glove.

Did I have them with me yesterday? I can't remember. If I did, then maybe it fell out of my pocket, she thought. Maybe it's in the car, or on the driveway.

With a shrug, Jennifer stuffed the single glove back in her pocket. She took another bite of apple and tossed it in the nearby garbage pail.

As she left the kitchen, the front doorbell rang. Still chewing, she pulled the door open.

Trisha stood on the porch, an anxious expression on her face. "Jen! Are you okay?" she demanded.

Jennifer swallowed quickly and pulled the door open wider. "Sure," she replied. "What are you doing here? I was supposed to pick *you* up, wasn't I?"

"Yes, but I couldn't wait," Trisha told her, stepping inside. "I had to come over. I had to make sure."

"Make sure of what?" Jennifer asked. "What are you talking about?"

Trisha glanced around nervously.

Jennifer frowned at her, confused. "Trisha, what's wrong?"

"I . . . I had another vision," Trisha murmured in a quick, nervous voice. "I saw another attack on Ty. But this time it was on his house."

An icy shiver ran up Jennifer's spine. I don't want to hear this, she thought. Please, don't tell me!

"I was in the attacker's head again," Trisha went on. "I saw what she did. But I also saw who she was!"

Jennifer's heart began to hammer. She laughed nervously. "Whoa. A split vision, huh?" she asked, trying to make a joke. "Did it make you cross-eyed?"

"Jen, listen to me!" Trisha insisted. She grabbed Jennifer's arm. "I *know* who it was! It was you. The attacker was you!"

Chapter Eight

"Are you crazy?" Jennifer backed away from Trisha, feeling stunned and betrayed.

I almost knew what she was going to say, Jennifer thought. But Trisha can't actually believe it. "Are you *crazy*?" she repeated.

Trisha sighed. "I wish I were."

"Well, what you just said is definitely nuts. I would never hurt anyone!" Jennifer cried.

"I know, but I saw it," Trisha insisted.

"So what? It was just a vision," Jennifer argued. "It didn't really happen."

Trisha glanced away from Jennifer, biting her lip nervously.

"What?" Jennifer demanded. "Tell me!"

Trisha took a deep breath. "It *did* happen. I heard it on the radio."

"Huh? What are you saying?"

"Someone set Ty Sullivan's house on fire last night," Trisha declared. "Ty was awake. He smelled the smoke and called the fire department. They got there in time to save most of the house and nobody was hurt. But, Jen—they say that someone set the fire on purpose."

Jennifer suddenly couldn't breathe. She felt dizzy, sick to her stomach.

"One of the fire trucks is still outside," Trisha said. "Didn't you hear the sirens or anything?"

Jennifer shook her head. "No. Nothing," she finally managed to choke out. She sucked in her breath. "I'm going over there."

"Jen . . ." Trisha said in a warning tone.

Jennifer cut her off. "I have to see." She brushed past Trisha and dashed out the front door.

"Jen, wait!" Trisha called, running after her.

"I have to see!" Jennifer repeated. She ran down the front steps and cut across the brown winter grass to the side yard.

The smell of smoke hung in the air.

Jennifer's heart sank. It *is* true, she thought. Someone tried to burn Ty's house down.

But not me. It couldn't have been me.

Or could it?

I dreamed about being in Ty's yard again, didn't I? I dreamed about walking through the hedge into his yard!

Did I really do it? Did I sleepwalk again?

Jennifer ran along the tall hedge until she came to the gap where the path led into Ty's yard. She paused at the opening, then walked quickly through the gap.

"Oh, no!" she breathed, shocked at the sight.

The back of Ty's house was blackened, almost to the roof. Ash sifted off the shingles and dusted the twisted stumps that had once been bushes.

Window glass littered the charred grass. Or what was left of it. Most of it had been churned into a mix of mud and ash.

The closed-in back porch had burned to the ground.

Jennifer moved a little closer, stopping next to a pile of blackened wood. Window frames, maybe.

"It's horrible, isn't it?" Trisha murmured, standing at Jennifer's side. "It's lucky nobody was killed."

Jennifer nodded. She couldn't speak.

I didn't do this, she thought. I could never do something like this.

She gazed across the yard and spotted

Greta and Jade and some other seniors. They milled around the ruined porch area, staring at the disaster with expressions of horror on their faces.

Ty wasn't with them.

Thank goodness, Jennifer thought. After what he said last night, *he* probably thinks I did this, too.

A fireman approached the other seniors and shooed them away. His thick yellow coat hung open. Smudges of soot stained his face and hands.

"See that woman?" Trisha asked.

Jennifer looked to the spot where Trisha was pointing. The woman wore a yellow hard-hat and stood with another fireman, examining a twisted shingle.

"I saw her when I first got here," Trisha said. "Jade told me that she's the arson investigator."

Arson. Jennifer shivered at the word.

"She's supposed to be able to tell how the fire started," Trisha went on. "Maybe there's gasoline or something on that shingle. Some kind of evidence." She glanced at Jennifer.

"It wasn't me, Trisha," Jennifer whispered desperately. "Your vision has to be wrong. Ty could have been killed! His parents, his little sister!"

An icy wind gusted as Jennifer gazed at the charred house. She crossed her arms and rubbed them. "Let's get out of here, okay? I'm cold."

As they turned away from the ruined house, Trisha stopped. "What's that?" she asked, staring at the pile of charred wood. She bent down and reached for something half-covered by a sooty board.

"Don't touch anything," Jennifer warned. "It might be evidence."

"Jen . . ." Trisha murmured in a shaken voice. She slowly straightened up. "Look."

Jennifer's scalp prickled. The blood began to pound in her ears and her mouth went dry.

Trisha held a glove in her hand. Part of it was charred black.

But the other part was lemon-yellow, with a pattern of tiny white snowflakes knitted into it.

It's mine, Jennifer gasped.

My lost glove.

Chapter Nine

Without thinking, Jennifer snatched the glove from Trisha's hand and stuffed it deep inside her jacket pocket.

Fear tightened her throat.

I didn't do it! she wanted to scream. I didn't set the fire! She touched the charred yellow glove in her pocket.

"It's yours, isn't it?" Trisha whispered. "Jennifer, how did it get here?"

Jennifer quickly shook her head. She didn't know how it got there!

But what about my dream? she reminded herself. I dreamed I was standing here, in Ty's backyard. My hands felt so cold.

Jennifer clenched her fists. Did I really come here? Did I take the gloves off to light the fire?

No! I couldn't have. I didn't do it! I would feel it if I did. I would know it!

Wouldn't I?

"Jen, we should go," Trisha whispered urgently, tugging on Jennifer's sleeve.

Jennifer nodded and began following Trisha out of the yard. When she reached the path, she glanced over her shoulder.

Her heart froze.

The arson investigator was staring at her.

Did she see me hide the glove?

The investigator broke the gaze and began talking to the fireman again.

Jennifer's knees felt weak. She swallowed and turned to Trisha. "Trisha, I'm scared!"

"Let's go someplace," Trisha said. "Get some breakfast and talk."

Jennifer nodded and followed Trisha to her car, the new white Corvette her parents had given her for Christmas.

Soon they were roaring down Fear Street. They turned onto Park Drive and drove to the Donut Hole.

Jennifer kept her voice low as they slid into a booth. "I do not understand what is happening to me."

"Jennifer, I think I—" Trisha started to say.

"Wait," Jennifer interrupted. "I have to tell you something. Last night, when I was driving home from basketball practice, I almost hit Ty."

Trisha's eyes grew wide.

"It was totally not my fault," Jennifer insisted. "You know how foggy it was. I didn't see him until the last second. I swerved, and I missed him. But Ty acted like I tried to run him down."

"What did he say?"

"He told me to keep away from him," Jennifer replied. "He was so angry. But it was an accident!"

Jennifer wrapped her hands around the thick mug of hot coffee. Her hands felt so cold.

The way they did when she woke up this morning.

"What did you do?" Trisha asked.

"Nothing. Ty ran off and I drove home." Jennifer sipped some coffee. "Then, this morning, I had the weird feeling that I'd been sleepwalking again. But my nightgown and slippers were dry and everything. I thought it was just a dream."

Trisha leaned forward, an intense expression on her face. "What was it about?"

Jennifer hesitated. "I had the feeling that I'd gone to Ty's backyard again." She tightened her fingers around the mug. "I was sure I didn't, Trisha! But now I'm really spooked. I don't know what's going on!"

"I think *I* do," Trisha declared.

Jennifer stared at her warily. Is Trisha

going to tell me about her vision again? That I set the fire? That I tried to kill Ty?

"Look, you know when all the weird things started happening, don't you?" Trisha asked.

Jennifer thought a couple of seconds. "I guess it was when Ty dumped me."

"No." Trisha shook her head. "It was when you got that necklace. That's when it started."

Startled, Jennifer reached up and touched the smooth red stone. "What does my new necklace have to do with anything?"

"Remember when I tried it on and saw that woman being hanged?" Trisha reminded her. "It was Dominique Fear, I'm sure of it. Because I kept on seeing her in my mind afterward. And the picture kept getting clearer. Finally I saw that she was wearing the same necklace."

Jennifer closed her hand around the garnet. "I don't get it," she said. "So what if the necklace was hers?"

"Don't you remember what I felt when I put it on?" Trisha asked. "I mean, what Dominique felt? Besides being scared."

Jennifer thought a second. "You said she was angry. Really furious."

"Exactly. The feeling was so strong. It was like pure hatred. Dominique was evil," Trisha declared. "That's what I felt."

Jennifer drew back, shocked. "You never said *that*."

"I know," Trisha admitted. "You were so happy with the necklace and everything. Why should I spoil it? I didn't know it would matter. But it does."

"What do you mean?" Jennifer demanded.

"Dominique's evil," Trisha repeated. "She's dead, but her spirit isn't."

Jennifer frowned. This is unbelievable.

But Trisha's visions are definitely no joke, she reminded herself.

"Dominique's spirit is alive," Trisha said. "I think she used that necklace to come back. To act out . . . through you."

"But why me?" Jennifer demanded. "I don't even believe—"

"Because you're like her," Trisha interrupted. "You're a Fear, right? So is she."

Fear.

The word hit Jennifer like a slap. "I can't help it," she protested. "What am I supposed to do? Change my name?"

Trisha pointed at Jennifer's throat. "You have to get rid of that necklace."

Jennifer rubbed her finger across the garnet. Trisha's words still echoed in her mind.

You're like her. You're a Fear. You're like her. You're a Fear.

"No!" Jennifer cried. "I may be a Fear, but I'm *not* like her. I'm not evil!"

The waitress behind the counter glanced over, a curious expression on her face.

Jennifer lowered her voice. "I don't believe it," she declared to Trisha in a whisper.

"Jennifer, I know it sounds crazy, but it's true," Trisha insisted. "It's the only possible explanation."

"It's stupid!" Jennifer argued. "I wouldn't attack Ty or set his house on fire. I *couldn't* have done it. I just couldn't!"

"*You* wouldn't. But Dominique would," Trisha insisted. "I told you, she's using you. You were sleepwalking and you woke up in his backyard. The very night he got attacked, remember?"

Jennifer's hands shook. How could she ever forget? A feeling of panic washed over her.

"And your glove," Trisha went on. "How did it get there?"

"What do you care, anyway?" Jennifer snapped. "What are you worried about? You're not a Fear. If anyone has to pay for what's going on, it will be me!"

"Jen . . ."

"Stop talking about it!" Jennifer cried. She shoved her chair back and jumped to her feet. "I don't want to hear any more!"

Before Trisha could say anything else, Jennifer turned and ran right out of the restaurant.

Jennifer's footsteps echoed in the empty hall as she hurried toward the gym for basketball practice that afternoon.

You're like her. You're a Fear.

The words kept rhythm with her steps.

She's evil. You're like her.

You're a Fear.

Jennifer stopped abruptly. I'm *not* like her! she thought. I didn't do anything to Ty.

I was sleepwalking because I was upset. Ty dumped me. Maybe, in my dream, I wanted to see him. Even tell him off for being such a creep.

But I didn't attack him.

What about the glove? she heard Trisha's voice asking. *How did it get in Ty's yard?*

Jennifer gave her head a quick shake and began walking again. Stop thinking about it, she told herself. Go to basketball practice and try to forget.

She'd groaned when the coach had called for another practice today—the last one of the vacation. Now she was glad. Maybe it would take her mind off things.

Jennifer heard voices up ahead. Stacy and Deirdre? she wondered, thinking of two other seniors on the team.

No.

As she started to round the corner, she spotted three of Shadyside's cheerleaders standing outside the gym door. Jade Feldman, Deirdre Palmer's twin sister, Dana—and Greta Bradley.

Jennifer eased back around the corner before anyone saw her. The last person she wanted to see was Ty's new girlfriend.

She let out a soft groan. Why did the cheerleaders have to practice today?

"Ty is lucky to be alive!" she heard Dana exclaim. "What if he hadn't been awake?"

"I know. He and his parents are okay, thank goodness," Greta said. "But his house is a total mess. I was over there this morning. The whole place smells like smoke. It's just disgusting."

"Do they know how the fire started yet?" Dana asked.

"No, but they think someone might have lit it on purpose," Greta replied.

Jennifer's breath caught in her throat.

"I still don't get it. Who would want to burn Ty's house down?" Jade demanded.

"Maybe an ex-girlfriend," Dana suggested with a laugh. "A *jealous* ex-girlfriend. There are plenty of them around, right?"

The others laughed with her, even Greta.

I guess Greta doesn't care that Ty fools around, Jennifer thought. Maybe that's why he likes her instead of me.

"Who's Ty's latest dumpee?" Dana asked.

"Jennifer Fear," Greta told her. "And he's already mad at her. She almost ran him down with her car the other night."

I can't believe it! Jennifer thought. Did Ty

58

actually tell her I did it on purpose?

"Whoa!" Dana exclaimed. "Did she really try to hit him?"

Jennifer's heart banged in her ears.

"Who knows?" Greta replied. "But Ty says she was really upset when he broke up with her."

"Yeah, but Jennifer wouldn't torch his house, would she?" Jade asked.

The gym door clanked open.

"Talk about revenge!" Dana declared.

The cheerleaders' voices faded as the door banged shut.

Jennifer leaned against the wall. Her breath came in short gasps.

I didn't do it! she thought frantically. I almost hit Ty, but that was an accident.

And I couldn't have set fire to his house!

Slowly she reached into her jacket pocket and grasped the yellow glove.

Swallowing nervously, she fingered the charred wool.

But if I didn't do it, then how do I explain this?

Chapter Ten

That evening Jennifer slowly opened the double door of her father's library and stepped inside.

A dark cavelike room, the library held hundreds of ancient, musty-smelling books.

All had belonged to the Fears.

Some of them were about things such as the dark arts and instructions on how to cast evil spells.

But Jennifer wasn't interested in spells.

She wanted to find out about Dominique Fear.

I have to, she thought. I need to know who she was. I have to find out if Trisha is right about Dominique.

That she was hanged. That she was evil.

Jennifer crossed to the massive wooden desk. Last week she saw her father studying a big book about the history of the Fears. She was pretty sure he put it back on one of the shelves behind the desk.

She turned on the desk lamp and began searching. It didn't take her long to find it. Thick, bound in cracked black leather, the book's title stood out in gold lettering.

The Fear Family—A Chronicle.

Jennifer tugged it out of the bookcase and put it on the desk. Sitting in the worn leather chair, she opened the book.

The handwriting changed as Jennifer flipped through the thick yellowed pages. Of course, she thought. Whenever someone died, someone else took up writing the history of the family.

The first entry was for 1860. Jennifer scanned the pages, but Dominique's name didn't come up.

The handwriting changed in 1863. Jennifer squinted at the small black lettering, looking for names. Charles . . . Mary . . . William . . . Neil . . . Dominique!

1863 - Born to Charles and Mary Fear, a daughter, Dominique.

Jennifer eagerly flipped ahead, scanning the pages as fast as she possibly could without missing anything. Dominique's name finally came up again in 1879.

The past year has been one of tremendous worry, the historian wrote. *Dominique's shameful affair with Nigel Fetherston is over. But it threatened to ruin our name and leave her in disgrace, with no man willing to have her.*

Whoa, Jennifer thought. Dominique had an affair when she was what? Fifteen. But girls got married a lot younger then.

The chronicle didn't say anything about that. It didn't even mention Dominique again until 1880, when it said she'd given birth to a boy.

Jennifer slowly turned the pages, looking for something more. She found it in the year 1882.

Dominique is dead, the chronicle stated. *Tried, convicted, and hanged for the murder of Nigel Fetherston.*

Jennifer gasped. Trisha was right, she thought. Dominique *was* put to death. But why did she kill her old boyfriend?

Jennifer kept reading.

Dominique had been seeing visions since she was a little girl, the chronicle said. And a couple of years after she married, she had one about Nigel. She saw him walking along a cliff. The rocks were wet and he slipped, falling a hundred feet to his death.

Dominique tried to warn Nigel. He wasn't home, so she told his wife, who called her crazy and threw her out of the house.

Then, a few days later, the vision came true. Nigel Fetherston fell from the cliff, just as Dominique had said he would.

Jennifer shivered and read on.

Nigel's wife accused Dominique of killing him.

The police believed Nigel's wife and arrested Dominique. She went on trial for murder.

The morning was cloudy and bitterly cold, Jennifer read from the chronicle. *They brought forth Dominique to the scaffold and asked if she wished to speak.*

"I am innocent!" she cried.

They slipped the noose over her head.

Her expression grew dark and bitter. Her eyes glowed with a fearsome rage. "Someone shall pay!" she warned in a voice tortured by hatred. "Someday, someone shall pay for my death!"

Jennifer gazed at the words in horror.

Dominique swore revenge, she realized. Maybe Trisha is right. Maybe Dominique is getting her revenge now. By acting out through me!

Because I'm a Fear.

Jennifer fingered the garnet pendant around her neck and shuddered. I can't let that happen, she thought. I have to do what Trisha said. I have to get rid of this necklace!

She rushed out of the library and up to her room.

There, Jennifer stood in front of her dresser mirror and gazed at her reflection. The garnet gleamed softly at her throat, catching the light.

I should never have put it on, Jennifer thought.

It belonged to a Fear.

Maybe Dominique was evil and maybe she wasn't. It doesn't make any difference.

She was a Fear.

So am I.

I can't help what my last name is. But I *can* get rid of this necklace.

Jennifer raised her hands to the clasp at the back of her neck. She squeezed the two little prongs and pulled.

The clasp stuck.

She tried again.

The chain still didn't open.

What's wrong? Jennifer slid the chain around until the clasp was at her throat. She leaned forward and peered into the mirror.

She examined the clasp and tried to open it once more, but it wouldn't budge.

What's the matter with this stupid thing?

Jennifer wiped her hands on her jeans and leaned closer to the mirror. She squeezed the two gold prongs harder and pulled.

Nothing happened.

I have to get it off of me! Jennifer thought,

panicking. I can't stand having it around my neck a second longer!

Tear it off, she told herself. Break the chain. I'm not going to wear it again anyway.

Jennifer grasped the chain in both hands and tugged, but the gold links did not break apart.

She tugged again and again.

A shudder of fear raced down Jennifer's back.

How can it be so strong?

Is it Dominique? Is the necklace evil, too?

Jennifer gazed at the pendant in the mirror. The stone seemed to glow a fiery red.

She kept tugging on the chain. The links cut into her hands and bit into her neck.

The chain held.

She pulled at it again, harder.

Harder.

Jennifer gasped. Burning pain shot through her as the gold dug into her neck.

Jennifer winced. The pain grew stronger. Her skin felt as if it were on fire.

"It won't come off!" she cried, tearing at the chain in panic. "It won't come off!"

have to get Dominique Fear's pendant off me!

Jennifer tightened her grip on the chain.

She squeezed her eyes shut and yanked as hard as she could.

The links dug into her palms and sawed at the skin on her neck.

She gritted her teeth.

Sweat broke out on her forehead.

Get it off! she thought. Get it off!

Jennifer tugged again. The pain burned stronger. She bit her lip and whimpered. Tears spurted from her eyes.

"Jennifer!"

She whirled around.

Her mother stood in the doorway of the

bedroom, a startled expression on her face. "What are you doing, honey? What's wrong?"

Jennifer swallowed hard, trying to force back her feeling of hysteria. "The necklace won't come off," she replied, blinking back the tears.

"Well, don't keep yanking at it like that. You'll break it." Mrs. Fear crossed the room. "It's very old, remember—it's probably just stuck."

Jennifer dropped her hands as her mother took hold of the necklace.

The clasp opened easily.

Jennifer sighed with relief. "Thanks," she said as her mother put the necklace on the dresser.

"Look at your neck!" Jennifer's mother cried. "You hurt yourself."

Jennifer stared in the mirror. She gasped when she saw the raw red ring that circled her neck, where the chain had bitten into the skin.

"Go put some ointment on it," her mother told her.

"Okay." Jennifer glanced down at her palms. More chain marks, seeping blood.

Jennifer quickly closed her hands so her mother wouldn't see.

"Why don't you ask your father to take a look at the necklace?" Mrs. Fear suggested. "The clasp might be bent just a tiny bit."

"Yeah. Okay." Jennifer faked a yawn. "I'm really wiped out. See you in the morning, Mom."

"Good night, honey." Her mother kissed her on the cheek, then left the room, closing the door behind her.

Jennifer wiped her palms with a tissue and stared at the necklace on the dresser.

It belonged to Dominique, she thought. And right before she died, Dominique swore to get revenge someday.

It's crazy, but it's true. Somehow, Dominique really has come alive through this necklace.

Jennifer picked up the pendant.

A chill ran through her body as the silky gold chain fell through her fingers. The deep red garnet gleamed in the light.

Like blood, Jennifer thought.

You cannot wear it anymore, she told herself. You have to get rid of it like Trisha said. Get it out of your sight.

Now!

She yanked open a drawer and pulled out a white sweatsock. After dropping the necklace inside, she twisted the top of the sock into a thick knot.

Mom and Dad will ask why I never wear it anymore, she realized. I'll have to come up with a good reason. Dad will probably be hurt.

But I can't help it.

I have to put the necklace away.

Jennifer pulled open the bottom drawer and stuffed the sock at the very back.

I have to get it out of my life for good.

She slammed the drawer shut with a bang.

Crowds of shoppers filled the mall the next morning. Jennifer threaded her way through them, feeling slightly anxious.

Tomorrow night was New Year's Eve.

She had tons of things to do for her party that day. Meet Trisha at the Party Place to buy noisemakers and crepe-paper streamers and stuff. Go to the supermarket for a few more cases of soda. Clean the house.

What else? Jennifer wondered. She had bought all the food. Trisha was coming over tonight to help decorate. All Jennifer had to do tomorrow was decide what to wear.

And wait for eight o'clock, when the party started.

Jennifer pushed through the door of the Party Place. She looked around for Trisha, but didn't see her.

The store was packed. Shoppers pawed through bins of party hats and combed the shelves for paper plates and cups.

Jennifer made her way to the right aisle and spotted Trisha loading a basket with horns and blowers. "Hi!"

Trisha turned and waved. "How many do you need?" she asked as Jennifer joined her.

"Twenty, maybe. But let's get extras." Jennifer grabbed a handful of noisemakers and dropped them into the shopping basket. "I did it," she declared. "I put the necklace away."

"Really?" Trisha glanced at her, relieved and curious. "What made you decide to do it?"

"I found this Fear family history in Dad's library and read about Dominique," Jennifer replied. "You were right about her, Trisha. She definitely had a major grudge. And when they hanged her, she swore she'd get even."

"What happened?" Trisha demanded. "Why was she hanged?"

Jennifer leaned against the shelf and told Trisha about what she'd read. "I don't know for sure if she killed Nigel or not," she said when she finished. "She swore she didn't, but nobody believed her."

"She must have been innocent," Trisha declared. "Why else would she want to get revenge? The whole thing was totally unfair."

"I guess you're right," Jennifer agreed. "But let's not talk about it anymore. It really creeps me out. I mean, I'm *related* to her."

"I can still feel her hate," Trisha murmured. "It was so strong." She shivered slightly.

"Yeah, well . . ." Jennifer still felt a little uneasy.

Trisha smiled. "Now maybe everything will get back to normal. "I was worried you were going to . . ."

"Kill someone?" Jennifer asked.

Trisha nodded.

"Like you said, *I* wouldn't. But Dominique would." Jennifer took a deep breath. "Not anymore, though. I'm never putting that necklace on again. It's totally over."

Jennifer left the mall an hour later, with a shopping bag in each hand. One bag held the party supplies, the other a midnight-blue velvet top that she bought at Rage.

Trisha was still shopping, but Jennifer had more errands to run.

Picking her way around patches of ice in the parking lot, she reached her car and unlocked the trunk.

It's going to be a new year, she thought. A fresh start.

She was glad that she was having a party. It would help take her mind off everything that had been happening.

As she dropped the bags inside, someone grabbed her arm.

Jennifer screamed.

"Shut up!" a voice snarled.

The hand tightened on Jennifer's arm and spun her around.

"Ty!" she gasped. "What are you doing?"

Ty glared at her. "I'm giving you a warning," he declared in a cold voice.

"What are you talking about?"

"Don't play dumb, okay? First, you attack me . . ."

"I didn't—"

"Shut up!" he yelled again, squeezing her arm painfully. "You attack me, then you try to run me over, then you set my house on fire. You're sick. But I should have known that. After all, you're a Fear."

Jennifer wanted to scream that it wasn't true. That she didn't try to run him over. That she didn't burn his house down.

But I can't, she thought.

Not after what I read about Dominique.

Ty grabbed Jennifer's shoulders and shook her frantically. "You better stay away from me, freak!"

"Let go of me!" she cried. She wrenched her arm free and slammed the trunk lid down.

She pushed her way past Ty, yanked open the driver's door, and slid behind the wheel.

Ty grabbed the door before she could close it. "I'm warning you," he repeated. "Stay away from me and my family. Or I'll make you pay."

He slammed the door so hard the car rocked. Then he stalked off through the parking lot.

Jennifer sat for a moment, too stunned to move.

He could be right. I might really have tried to kill him.

Dominique swore revenge.

But it's over now.

I'm never wearing that necklace.

Nothing bad will happen again.

Then Jennifer had a terrifying thought. What if Dominique can make me do horrible things even if I'm *not* wearing the necklace?

After all, we have a bond.

We're Fears.

Jennifer shook her head, trying to push the awful idea from her mind. A lump rose in her throat, almost choking her.

Frightened and miserable, Jennifer leaned her forehead on the steering wheel and sobbed. "Please let it be over. Please."

Chapter Twelve

"There!" Trisha exclaimed as she hung a gold and silver Happy New Year banner over the doorway of Jennifer's living room. "Everything's ready."

Jennifer glanced around. Streams of crepe paper decorated the window frames. Gold and silver balloons clung to the ceiling. The noisemakers sat in a basket on a table next to the door.

The dining room, through an archway, had the same decorations. Jennifer and Trisha had already covered a big table with a paper cloth and stacked piles of napkins on it. Tomorrow night the table would be filled with food and drinks.

Trisha climbed down from the step stool.

"It looks great, Jen. It's going to be so much fun."

Jennifer sighed.

"Jen! You've been totally silent all night," Trisha declared. "What's wrong?"

"I keep trying to forget, but . . ." Jennifer's throat closed up and tears filled her eyes.

"But what?" Trisha demanded, concerned. "What are you talking about?"

"Ty!" Jennifer burst out. She wiped her eyes and took a deep breath. Then she told Trisha about the encounter with Ty in the parking lot. "He's positive I'm out to get him! And I can't stop thinking about the glove and everything. And what I read about Dominique. I'm so afraid."

"But it's over," Trisha reminded her. "You took the necklace off."

"I know, but what if that wasn't enough?" Jennifer demanded. "What if Dominique still controls me somehow?"

Trisha thought a moment. "Remember when I put the necklace on that time?" she said slowly. "Why don't I wear it again and see what happens?"

"Like what?" Jennifer asked doubtfully.

"Like whether her spirit's dead now," Trisha replied. "I mean, if nothing happens, we know that attacking Ty and burning his house was enough revenge for her, right?"

Jennifer hesitated. The necklace spooked

her. "What if it wasn't enough?" she asked. "What if her spirit is still alive?"

"*I'll* be wearing the necklace, not you," Trisha reminded her. "She used you because you're a Fear. But nothing will happen if I wear it."

"Well . . . okay," Jennifer agreed reluctantly. "Let's try it."

Jennifer led the way upstairs to her bedroom and dug out the sock from the dresser drawer. She untied the knot and spilled the gold and garnet necklace into her palm. "Here."

Trisha slowly took the necklace and draped it around her throat. She tilted her head and swept her hair to the side.

Jennifer fastened the clasp for her and stepped away.

Trisha turned around. "See? There's . . . "

Her face turned a ghostly white. Her eyes went blank like before. Like when she was seeing one of her visions.

Jennifer gasped. "Trisha!"

Trisha did not respond.

Slowly Trisha began to change. The color returned to her face. Her shoulders drew back and she stood straighter.

She looks almost like a different person, Jennifer thought. Not so small and delicate. She actually looks taller.

Stronger.

Trisha's hands suddenly curled into fists.
She lifted her chin. The cords in her neck
stood out. Her lips twisted.

"Someone shall pay!" she cried. "Someday,
someone shall pay for my death!"

Chapter Thirteen

"**S**omeone shall pay!" Trisha repeated. Her voice was raw and tortured.

Filled with hate.

Those were Dominique's words. Jennifer gasped. The exact words she said before they hanged her!

It's Dominique's voice, Jennifer realized. Just the way the chronicle described it.

Her spirit isn't dead. It's still alive.

And Dominique has taken over Trisha's body.

She's speaking to me through Trisha.

"It was so easy for them to accuse me," Trisha declared. She raised her hand and touched the garnet. "It is easy to condemn a Fear. And even easier to hang one!"

Trisha's face softened for a moment. Her

eyes glowed. "Nigel Fetherston was the world to me. So handsome with his strong jaw and golden hair. I thought he loved me. I thought he would marry me. What a fool I was!"

Trisha laughed bitterly. "When I asked him if we would marry, he laughed. He would never marry a Fear!"

Trisha's lip curled, as if she were imitating Nigel's expression. She shook her head and began to pace the room.

Jennifer stepped out of her way. The backs of her knees hit the bed and she sat, never taking her eyes from Trisha.

"The entire town knew of our affair," Trisha continued. "And when Nigel died, they believed I killed him. They believed me to be jealous and vengeful because he wouldn't marry me."

Jennifer sat tensely, waiting. She didn't know what else to do.

"It was a lie!" Trisha cried. "I tried to warn him! I saw him in a vision, falling from the cliff. I heard him scream in terror. I heard the hideous sound of his bones cracking on the rocks below."

Trisha covered her ears, as if she could still hear the sound.

"It was a vision," she whispered. "But no one believed me. I was a Fear. I must be lying. They pronounced me guilty. Guilty. *Guilty!*"

Jennifer felt her heart pounding as Trisha waved a fist in the air.

"They hanged me," Trisha said through clenched teeth. "And because I was a Fear, they did not dare contaminate holy ground. They buried me in the woods, *behind* the cemetery."

Trisha's eyes glittered maliciously. "I need a Fear to get my revenge. And I shall *have* my revenge." She locked her eyes onto Jennifer. Her expression grew dark and hateful. "With you!"

Jennifer cried out as Trisha lunged toward her.

Chapter Fourteen

Jennifer screamed again as she bounded off the bed. "Trisha, noooo!"

"Someone shall pay!" Trisha repeated. "I will . . ."

Trisha's voice rose to a shrill cry.

Jennifer gasped.

The color suddenly drained from Trisha's face. She gasped for breath. Her eyes rolled back in her head.

"Trisha!" Jennifer cried as she watched her friend collapse to the floor.

Jennifer rushed across the room. Knelt down and grabbed Trisha's hand.

Ice cold.

"Trisha!" Jennifer brushed her friend's blond hair out of her eyes and peered into her face. "Trisha, wake up! Come out of it, please!"

Trisha didn't stir.

Jennifer started to yell for help when the necklace caught her eye.

Dominique's necklace. Maybe Trisha is still under Dominique's spell.

Frantically, Jennifer turned Trisha's head to the side and fumbled for the clasp. Her fingers trembled, but she finally managed to squeeze the prongs.

The clasp slid open.

Jennifer lifted Trisha's head and yanked the necklace off, tossing it across the room. "Trisha? Can you hear me?"

Trisha moaned softly. Her eyelids fluttered, then opened wide. She stared up at Jennifer. "I feel so . . . weird," she murmured.

Jennifer sighed with relief. Dominique wouldn't use the word *weird*.

Trisha was back.

"Are you all right?" Jennifer asked. She helped Trisha sit up. "Do you remember what happened?"

Trisha shook her head and rubbed a hand across her face. "I remember feeling sad. And scared. Then furious. Really, really furious!"

"You actually *became* Dominique," Jennifer declared. "Totally. The way you talked and walked and everything. You were a completely different person. It was so creepy!"

Trisha frowned. "What did I say?"

"You talked about Nigel and how he died,"

Jennifer told her. "How they hanged you for it. You said the exact same words I read in the book—'Someday, someone shall pay.' I thought you meant Nigel, but then you came after me!"

"What?" Trisha cried. "Are you okay?"

Jennifer nodded. "But I'm scared, Trish. I mean, Dominique took over your *body!* That means she used me, too!" Jennifer gasped at the horror of it all. "Dominique was inside my head," she said. "All this time I didn't think I could hurt someone. But I did. I tried to kill Ty!"

Trisha glanced across the room.

Jennifer followed her gaze and shivered. The necklace had landed in a corner, a small heap of red and gold. "Dominique's spirit is *not* dead," she added. "She wants more revenge. And she's going to use me to get it. To kill!"

"I felt her rage, I remember that much." Trisha gazed into Jennifer's eyes. "She is definitely dangerous."

Jennifer jumped to her feet, rubbing her arms nervously. She crossed the room and scooped up the necklace. "I'm putting this away again. It's evil."

"Good idea," Trisha said, following Jennifer with her eyes. "I bet all her power is in that necklace. She can only use you if you wear it, right?"

If only I had never gotten it in the first place, Jennifer thought. She stared at the necklace. "I wish I'd never touched it or worn it or even *see* it."

But it was too late for that.

Jennifer crossed to the dresser and picked up the sweatsock. She dropped the necklace back into it and knotted the sock. Then stuffed it at the back of the drawer again.

"There." Jennifer slammed the drawer shut and glanced at Trisha. "Everything will be okay now. Right?"

Chapter Fifteen

"**H**ey, Jennifer!" someone yelled.

Jennifer jumped, frightened at first, then turned around. She couldn't get her mind off what had happened the night before. She was even going to cancel the party, but Trisha had convinced her not to.

A noisemaker uncurled and bopped her in the nose.

"Happy New Year!" Matty Winger shouted in her face. He blew the noisemaker again. *Whonk! Whonk!*

Jennifer rolled her eyes and batted the noisemaker aside. "Having fun, Matty?"

"Hey, what do you think? Great party, Jen. Awesome!" Matty grabbed one more noisemaker from the basket and stuck both of them in his mouth. Looking a little like a walrus, he headed across the living room to bother somebody else.

Jennifer rolled her eyes again. Trust Matty to act like a total idiot. Oh, well. It *is* New Year's Eve.

And the party is going great, she thought. She gazed around the living room.

Just relax, Jen, she told herself.

A pounding drumbeat shook the floor. Kids danced to the music or stood in groups, talking loudly.

More kids crowded the dining room, scarfing down chips and dip and hunks of the two five-foot submarine sandwiches.

Noisemakers honked every few seconds. Shouts of laughter rose over the music.

The new year was less than two hours away.

It's a good thing Mom and Dad went to somebody else's house for a party, Jennifer told herself as she began weaving her way through the living room. This one is way too loud for them.

Stacy Malcolm caught Jennifer's arm as she passed by. "Cool party, Jen."

"Yeah, it's really fun," Josie Maxwell agreed.

"Thanks." Jennifer glanced at their heads. Both wore party hats, colorful cones with glued-on sparkles and elastic bands under their chins.

"Where did you get those?" Jennifer asked. "I didn't buy any hats."

"I brought them," Stacy told her with a grin.

Jennifer laughed. Stacy almost always wore a hat, the funkier, the better. "I better go check the food supply," she said. "Catch you guys later."

As she made her way toward the dining room, Kenny Klein bumped into her. He jumped back, sloshing half his drink onto the carpet.

"Whoa!" Kenny cried. He held the dripping cup out to his side. "Oh, man. I'm sorry, Jennifer."

"Forget about it," she told him. "It's the same color as the rug. Once it dries, nobody will know."

Kenny laughed and ran a hand over his dark brown hair. "Whatever you say."

Jennifer gazed around the room, looking for Kenny's girlfriend. They usually stuck together. "Where's Jade?" she asked. "I haven't seen her yet."

Kenny made a face. "Strep throat."

"Oh, too bad. Well, I'm glad you could come anyway."

"Me, too. Hey, you and I have to dance at least once before midnight," Kenny declared.

"Definitely," Jennifer agreed. She really liked Kenny. He was the smartest guy in the senior class, and one of the nicest. "Just let me see if the food's running out yet."

She waved goodbye to Kenny and worked her way toward the dining room archway.

Phoebe Yamura was in one corner talking to Josh Maxwell, Josie's stepbrother.

Jennifer watched Josh for a few seconds. His old girlfriend, Debra Lake, had been murdered the month before. Mira Block, another senior, went psycho and killed her. Josh and Debra had already broken up, but even so, Josh took it pretty hard.

And he still looks a little stressed, Jennifer thought. At least he's here, though.

Trisha spotted Jennifer and waved. She handed her glass to her boyfriend, Gary, then hurried over to the doorway. "Jen, this party is going great, isn't it?" she exclaimed.

"It really is," Jennifer agreed, smiling. "Is Gary having a good time?"

"Everybody is," Trisha replied.

Jennifer stood on tiptoe and checked out the table. Still plenty of drinks. But one of the subs was totally demolished. And only half the second one remained.

"I better get the third sub," Jennifer said.

Trisha suddenly clutched Jennifer's arm. "What's *she* doing here?"

"What? Who?" Jennifer turned and looked.

Greta stood in the door of the living room.

Ty stood next to her, one arm draped around her shoulders.

Jennifer stared in shock. I can't believe

this! she thought. Why would Ty show up at my party? He thinks I'm trying to kill him!

"Did you actually invite Greta?" Trisha demanded.

"I invited everybody," Jennifer reminded her. She couldn't take her eyes off the couple. "But that was before Ty dumped me. I can't believe he came."

"*And* brought his new girlfriend," Trisha added coldly. "You should kick her out. She doesn't have any business being here."

Jennifer kept staring, still stunned. What should I do? she wondered. Should I really say something to them or just pretend it doesn't matter?

Matty Winger elbowed his way to Ty and Greta and blew his noisemakers in their faces. Greta gave him a cool smile. Ty laughed. Both of them began to pull off their jackets.

They're really staying, Jennifer thought, amazed. "Maybe Ty decided I'm not out to get him after all," she murmured to Trisha. "Anyway, I'm not going to make a big deal out of this."

Trisha frowned. "Why not? It's your house."

"I know, but I don't want a major scene or anything," Jennifer told her.

Trisha nodded slowly. "I guess you're right. Why should you let them ruin your party?"

"Exactly." Jennifer shook off the feeling of shock and hurried into the kitchen. She hefted the third submarine sandwich from the table and carried it to the dining room.

Kenny Klein appeared as she finished cutting the sub into slices. "Sixty minutes and counting," he announced, taking her hand. "Let's dance!"

In the living room the floor vibrated as people danced to the loud, pulsing music. Jennifer and Kenny joined in, spinning around and bumping elbows with the crowd.

Someone turned the volume up on the music.

Jennifer's face grew hot and her hair felt sweaty at the base of her neck.

Kenny laughed and danced even faster as the beat picked up.

Jennifer's cheeks burned and she felt breathless. Her new velvet top began to feel like a blanket.

Kenny's face blurred.

The room swirled around her and began to tilt.

The music ended.

Jennifer took a few deep breaths and fanned her face with her hand. Her pulse was racing and she still felt dizzy.

The music started up again.

"One more?" Kenny asked.

The room had stopped swaying, but

Jennifer still felt weird. Not like herself. "Maybe later," she said.

Kenny turned to dance with someone else. Jennifer made her way out of the living room and pulled open the front door.

A draft of winter air blew in, cooling her face.

She stepped outside to the porch, pulling the door nearly closed behind her, then leaned against the railing. She lifted her hair and let the cold night air blow across the back of her neck. She watched as snowflakes formed a white blanket across the front lawn.

The music ended.

Jennifer heard everyone laughing and talking, and she smiled to herself. The party's great, even with Ty showing up. Maybe my life is getting back to normal—now that I know how to keep Dominique away from me.

She tilted her head and gazed at the snowflakes fluttering to the ground. I should go back in, she thought. But everything's so peaceful.

Jennifer closed her eyes and breathed deeply. Just another minute, she thought. Then I'll . . .

A piercing scream ripped through the night.

Terror jolted through Jennifer's body.

That's Trisha's scream! she realized.

Something happened to Trisha!

Panicked, Jennifer threw herself toward the door and shoved it open.

A bunch of kids were already on the stairs, yelling questions as they ran up toward the second floor.

"Who *was* that?"

"What's going on?"

"Somebody sure likes to party hard!"

Jennifer pounded up after them, frantic to get to her friend. She has to be hurt. Why else would she scream like that?

She reached the second floor and stared down the hall. More kids were gathered around the door of the guest bedroom, where everyone had put their coats. They craned their necks, trying to see inside.

Jennifer hurried down the hall, pushing her way through the crowd.

As she stumbled into the guest bedroom, she saw Kenny Klein.

And Trisha.

Jennifer started to cry out with relief, but the expressions on her friends' faces stopped her.

They were staring, horrified, at something on the floor.

Jennifer glanced down and felt a wave of panic flood through her.

Greta lay on the carpet in a pool of blood.

Dead.

Chapter Sixteen

Jennifer gasped as she stared at Greta's lifeless body.

She was crumpled on her side, with one arm flung out.

Her eyes stared blankly at the wall.

Blood streamed through her blond hair and across her face, soaking into the tan carpet under her head.

She didn't move.

Didn't breathe.

Small pieces of bright blue ceramic were scattered across the floor. A larger chunk, stained with blood, lay near Greta's head.

Mom's bowl, Jennifer realized. The one she bought in Mexico. It smashed onto Greta's head and . . .

Someone moaned behind her.

Jennifer whirled around.

Ty stood in the doorway, staring at Greta. Slowly he raised his eyes and stared at Jennifer. "You did this," he muttered in a choked voice.

The other kids gasped.

"No!" Jennifer cried. She turned her gaze to Greta again.

"I came upstairs a few minutes ago to look for Greta. I saw someone run out of this room. It was you! I'm sure of it!"

"No!" Jennifer cried again. "I didn't . . . I didn't do anything!"

I was dancing with Kenny, she remembered. I felt dizzy and went outside. How could I hurt Greta?

Unless . . .

The room began to spin.

Jennifer's stomach churned. Clapping a hand over her mouth, she stumbled across the floor into the guest bathroom. Leaned against the toilet. And threw up.

Trisha entered as Jennifer was splashing water on her face.

"Are you okay?" Trisha asked. "Do you know what happened?"

Jennifer snapped her head up. "I didn't do it!" she cried, staring at Trisha's reflection in the mirror. "I swear I didn't!"

"Maybe you didn't," Trisha said.

"*Maybe?* What's that supposed to mean?" Jennifer demanded.

"What about Dominique?" Trisha asked. "She could have done it. Maybe . . ."

No! Jennifer thought. It isn't true. She shook her head violently. "It wasn't her and it wasn't me," Jennifer said. "I was dancing with Kenny and then I went outside. I didn't come up here until I heard you scream! Besides, I'm not even wearing the necklace."

"Jen, I . . ." Trisha started to say.

Someone rapped on the door. Trisha pulled it open.

Two police officers stood outside.

Jennifer tried not to panic. Greta's dead. Of course somebody had to call the police. It doesn't mean they think I killed her. How could they?

She wiped her face on a towel and stepped into the bedroom. Trisha followed.

The other kids had left the room, taking their coats with them. Jennifer could hear them talking downstairs.

A man knelt next to Greta's body, examining her. Jennifer swallowed and glanced away.

"Just a few questions," one of the officers told her.

Jennifer nodded. She kept her eyes on his face, afraid to look at Greta again.

The policeman asked her name and

Greta's name and where Jennifer's parents were. "They're at a party at some friends' house," she told him in a shaky voice. She gave him the number.

He jotted it down and told his partner to call. "Can you tell us what happened?" he asked Jennifer.

"No, I . . ." Jennifer turned to Trisha.

"Kenny and I came upstairs to get some more CDs," Trisha explained. "Not in here, down the hall. Anyway, I just sort of glanced in and . . . saw her."

"You didn't see anyone else?" the officer asked.

Trisha slowly shook her head.

He nodded. Then he turned and stared across the room.

Jennifer followed his gaze. The high shelf where her mother kept the heavy ceramic bowl hung by only one bracket. The rest of it swung loose against the wall.

The shelf fell, Jennifer realized. I didn't see it before. Ty probably didn't, either. Maybe Greta slammed the door or maybe the music made the walls vibrate. But the shelf fell.

It *was* an accident.

Relief flooded through her. Don't be so selfish, she told herself.

Greta's dead.

You should not be happy, Jennifer told herself.

But she was—happy to know that she didn't kill Greta. She couldn't help feeling glad about that.

The policeman interrupted Jennifer's thoughts. "We're going to have more questions, but that's it for now."

"Okay. Thank you." Jennifer forced herself to look at Greta again. The cheerleader's body was on a stretcher now, completely covered with a thick white sheet. Two medical workers carried her out of the room.

Then a police officer led them outside the room and closed the door. He ran yellow tape across the door. The words CRIME SCENE were printed on it. "Don't go back in there until we tell you it's okay," he said.

Jennifer and Trisha followed the police and the stretcher downstairs. As she shut the door after them, Jennifer heard a choked sob.

She turned around.

Ty stood in front of her.

Tears filled his eyes. Jennifer could see his throat muscles working as he tried to force back another sob.

"It's awful, Ty," Jennifer murmured. "I know you're upset. It was an awful, terrible accident."

Ty exploded, his face turning a deep, angry red. "You think I believe that?" he shouted.

Jennifer flinched, shocked and frightened by his fury.

"It was no accident," Ty declared bitterly as the tears ran down his face. "You're jealous because I dumped you. You wanted to pay me back. You tried to run me down. Torched my house. And now—you murdered my girlfriend!"

"No!" Jennifer cried. "You don't know what you're talking about. The shelf fell and the bowl hit Greta's head. The police wouldn't just leave if they thought it was murder!"

"Yeah? Well, maybe you fooled the police, but you can't fool me," Ty snarled. "I know what you are. You're a Fear. A sick, twisted killer!"

Before Jennifer could respond, Ty bolted past her. He stormed out of the house and slammed the door so hard that the walls shuddered.

Jennifer wrapped her arms around herself and stared at the door. "I didn't do it!" she cried. "I know I didn't!"

Someone coughed.

Jennifer glanced around.

Everyone was in the hall, zipping their jackets and moving toward the door.

Totally silent, they edged past Jennifer and quickly left the house.

No one met her eyes.

Jennifer felt helpless. She turned to

Trisha, the only one who stayed behind. "Did you see that?" she asked. "The way they wouldn't look at me? They can't believe Ty, can they? They must have seen the shelf. It was an accident."

Trisha hunched her shoulders and stared at the floor. "It wasn't," she murmured. "I'm sorry, Jen. But it wasn't an accident."

"Wh-what do you mean?" Jennifer stammered. "You said you didn't see anyone."

"I lied to the police," Trisha whispered. "I *did* see something. I had another vision and I saw it happen. I saw the killer's hands pull down the shelf."

Slowly Trisha raised her head and stared at Jennifer. Her eyes were filled with fear. And pity.

Jennifer's breath caught in her throat. "You mean you saw *my* hands, didn't you? But how? I *know* it wasn't me! How could you see my hands?"

"I just . . ." Trisha hesitated. "I can't deal with this." She hurried out the door, leaving Jennifer alone in the empty house.

Jennifer couldn't move. Images of her dreams flooded her mind. Sleepwalking into Ty's backyard. Setting his house on fire.

This can't be happening, Jennifer thought. Could Dominique really take over my body? When I'm awake? When I'm not even wearing her necklace?

Did she make me . . . kill Greta?

Jennifer's heart pounded harder. We're bonded by our name.

Fear.

She tried to take a deep breath, but she just couldn't. What am I going to do? she wondered desperately.

What am I going to do?

A horn honked loudly.

A loud boom echoed through the night. More horns honked. Strings of firecrackers popped.

Happy New Year, Jennifer thought.

Happy New Year from Dominique.

Jennifer started to laugh hysterically. The laughter changed to sobs. Tears spilled from her eyes.

She raced onto the porch, gulping in huge breaths of cold air. "Leave me alone!" she screamed into the night. "Dominique, leave me alone!"

Chapter Seventeen

Jennifer stood in front of her dresser the next morning and stared into the mirror.

Her eyes had dark smudges under them. Her skin was pale and sick-looking. Her hand shook as she pulled the brush through her hair.

She'd only dozed during the night. She jerked awake every few minutes, her heart pounding.

Did I sleepwalk again?

Did I kill again?

The hairbrush slipped, banging painfully against her temple. She slammed it onto the dresser and hurried downstairs.

Her parents sat at the breakfast table. They were talking in low, worried voices. Her mother spotted Jennifer and quickly stood up. "Honey, how are you?" she asked. "You look exhausted. Sit down, I'll get you some juice." Mrs. Fear rose from her chair and grabbed a pitcher on the kitchen counter.

Jennifer pulled out a chair and collapsed into it.

Her father patted her arm. "We're so sorry about what happened," he told her. "It's a terrible tragedy, and we know you feel guilty. But you have to keep telling yourself you aren't responsible."

"Maybe I am," Jennifer muttered.

"Jennifer, of course you're not!" her mother exclaimed. "The police are still investigating, but they're going to find it was an accident. The shelf just . . . fell."

"Yeah, but the police don't really know everything," Jennifer declared.

Mrs. Fear frowned. A small crease appeared in between her eyebrows. She set down the juice pitcher on the table and clasped her hands together. "Jennifer, I don't understand."

"What are you saying, Jennifer?" Mr. Fear asked. "You don't expect us to believe that you had anything to do with that girl's death, do you?"

"I don't *know*. Maybe I did. I just don't know!" Jennifer cried. She scraped back her chair and stood up. She couldn't talk about this sitting down.

She crossed to the counter and braced herself against it, facing her parents. Then she told them everything that had happened. Everything since the day she received the necklace.

She talked about Ty and how he was attacked. How she almost hit him with her car. How she'd found her burned glove in his yard the day after the fire.

She told them about her dreams. About sleepwalking.

About Trisha putting on the necklace and reliving the story of Dominique Fear.

"I know it sounds crazy, but Dominique has come alive through that necklace," Jennifer said. "Through *me*. She used me to kill! I put the necklace away, but it didn't help. Because last night Trisha had another vision. She saw Greta's death. And she saw *my* hands pulling that shelf down over Greta's head!"

Jennifer sank down to the kitchen floor and cried. Her parents watched her with stunned expressions.

"I never believed in the legend before. About how the Fears were horrible, evil people," Jennifer said between sobs. "But I'm so scared. I mean, Dominique used me to kill. Just because I'm a Fear!"

Jennifer stopped talking and stared at her concerned parents' faces.

I shouldn't have said anything, she thought. There's nothing they can do about our name.

"Jennifer . . ." Mr. Fear cleared his throat. "There's something I have to tell you." He glanced at his wife. "Both of you."

"What?" Jennifer asked.

Mr. Fear cleared his throat again.

He's nervous, Jennifer realized. His face is red, like he's ashamed or something.

"It's about our last name," he said. "It's not really . . . well, it's not really Fear."

Jennifer's mother gasped.

Jennifer just stared at her father, totally shocked.

"When your grandfather moved to Shadyside, he was on his own. Parents dead, no other relatives," he told her. "The name Fear was big in town. If you were a Fear, people did you favors. Got you in the door at businesses. Got you into the country club, no questions asked. And your grandfather wanted all those things. So . . . he took the name Fear for himself."

Jennifer still couldn't speak.

"He never told my mother," Mr. Fear went on. "And he only told me right before he died. By then the charade had gone on so long, I decided just to let things be. And then you, your mother, and I moved back to Shadyside—"

"You mean none of us are related to the Fears?" Jennifer's mother asked in a dazed tone.

He shook his head, a sheepish expression on his face.

"What about all that stuff in the library?" Jennifer asked. "The spell books? The Fear chronicle? Why did you put so much effort into finding those things?"

"It's just a hobby," her father said, smiling weakly.

We're not Fears, Jennifer thought. The whole thing is a total lie.

A bubble of laughter rose in her throat. She tried to choke it back, but it burst out. And then she couldn't stop herself. She laughed hysterically, gasping for breath.

"I'm not a Fear!" she cried. "I'm not a Fear!"

Still laughing, she rose to her feet, raced upstairs, and dug the old sweatsock out of the drawer to her dresser. She shook the necklace into her palm and ran back down to the kitchen.

"Take it!" she cried, holding it out to her father. Her laughter turned bitter. "I don't want it. I never want to see it again, or anything to do with the Fears. Don't you know what it's been like for me? Everybody giving me weird looks whenever something bad happens, just because of my last *name?*"

"I'm sorry, Jennifer," her father told her. "I

don't blame you for being upset."

"Upset?" Jennifer replied. "When I was little the kids wouldn't play with me because they were afraid. Then we got older and they started teasing me. Taunting me because I'm a Fear. And it hasn't stopped. It will never stop. How could you do this to me? You've ruined my life!"

"I know it's been hard for you," Mr. Fear said. "Put the necklace in the library. I'll take care of it."

"Why not put it in the garbage?" Jennifer shouted angrily. "That's where it belongs!"

"Honey, don't say that," her mother pleaded.

"You can't possibly believe it has any real powers," her father added. "Just put it in the library and we'll forget all about it."

"I'll never forget it!" Jennifer cried. She raced from the kitchen through the long winding halls to her father's library.

She flung open the double door and burst inside, panting.

With a cry, she threw the necklace across the floor. It skittered under a low table and pinged against the stone hearth of their fireplace.

She gazed around the room, hating the place. Hating the Fears.

"I'm not one of you!" she cried. "I hate you. *Hate* you!"

Sizzling with anger, Jennifer stormed to a shelf, yanked out an old leather volume, and heaved it across the room.

The spine cracked as the book landed with a thud. Pages scattered across the floor.

Jennifer smiled grimly. It feels good to destroy this horrible stuff, she thought.

So why stop with one book?

She grabbed more books and flung them to the ground.

She marched to the fireplace and swept a pair of tarnished brass candlesticks off the mantel. They banged onto the hearth and rolled out onto the floor.

She kicked one across the room.

"I'm not one of you!" she repeated, kicking the other candlestick. "Do you hear that, Dominique? I'm not a Fear!" she shouted.

Frustrated and still angry, she pulled another handful of books off a shelf and threw them to the ground.

"I'm not a Fear!" she cried again, kicking one of the books.

Then she stopped.

"Wait a minute," she said under her breath. She wiped her sweaty forehead with the back of her hand.

Dominique took over my body, made me do evil things, she thought.

Because I was wearing her necklace.

And because we had a bond.

The name Fear.

Jennifer glanced around the Fear family library. The place was a wreck. Papers and books were scattered across the entire floor.

So then why is this happening?

Why is Dominique possessing me *if I'm not even a Fear?*

Chapter Eighteen

Jennifer started to kick another book, then caught herself.

I can destroy everything in this room, and it won't make any difference, she thought.

I still killed Greta.

Dominique is still using *me* to get her revenge.

Trisha thinks it's because I'm a Fear. But that's not true.

All I know is that I have to stop Dominique. But will I be able to?

Jennifer took a deep, shaky breath. She wiped her eyes and gazed around the room again.

It looked like a small tornado hit it. With a

sigh she waded through all the books and loosened pages and picked up the ugly brass candlesticks. She set them back up on the mantel, then bent down for the necklace.

Dad said he'd take care of it. I wonder what that meant.

She glanced around for a place to put the necklace. The desk drawer, she decided. She carried the necklace across the room, holding it by the garnet.

The stone felt loose under her thumb.

It must have happened when I threw it, she thought.

She sat on the heavy wooden desktop and checked the garnet out. Definitely loose.

Maybe I should just pull it out and smash it with a hammer.

Slipping her fingernail between the stone and the gold backing, Jennifer carefully pried the garnet free and set it on the desk.

Beneath the garnet was a thin sheet of gold with a tiny hinge on one side.

A hidden compartment, Jennifer realized.

Using her fingernail again, Jennifer pried the tiny door open.

Whoa.

A lock of dark hair, threaded with a faded yellow satin cord, lay curled up inside the compartment.

Jennifer lifted it out, letting it uncoil between her fingers.

It still felt soft. Silky. As if it had just been cut. Jennifer shuddered.

This was in here for a long time. It probably belongs to a dead person, she thought. Is it Dominique's?

Maybe it's Nigel's. Maybe she kept his hair even after he dumped her. But no. Dominique had told them—speaking through Trisha—that Nigel had golden hair.

Jennifer shuddered again and put the coil of hair back into the necklace.

She closed the compartment and replaced the garnet as well as she could. Then she hopped off the desk and left the library.

The kitchen was empty. Good. Jennifer still didn't feel like talking to her father.

I might never talk to him again, she thought. Not after the way he lied to me.

She picked up the phone and punched in Trisha's private number. Wait till she hears I'm not a Fear, she thought.

Trisha's answering machine clicked on. Jennifer hung up and tried the main number.

The maid answered. "Trisha isn't here at the moment," she told Jennifer. "Do you want to leave a message?"

Jennifer smiled dryly. Tell her I'm not who I thought I was, she said to herself. "No, thanks," she told the maid. "I'll call again in a little while."

Back in the Fear library, Jennifer began

picking up the books. She shoved them onto the shelves, not caring if they were in the right place.

No way will I ever be reading them, she thought.

Maybe Dad won't either anymore. How could he even keep them all this time when he knew he wasn't a Fear? What a weird hobby.

Sneezing from the dust, she gathered up the pages that had scattered across the floor. She shuffled them together without checking the order and stuffed them into the broken binding.

Spells to Cast Out Evil, the title read.

Jennifer bit her lip. Now she hated this Dark Arts stuff even more than she did before.

But this book is different, Jennifer thought. This tells how to get *rid* of evil.

It won't hurt to look, she decided. If Dominique can control me, why shouldn't I try anything to get rid of her?

Jennifer hauled the heavy book over to the desk and opened it, looking for a table of contents or something.

A thin tissue-like paper covered the title page. Beneath it she glimpsed what looked like a sketch. She lifted the paper—a thick parchment.

The drawing showed a house. A mansion, actually. A huge place, sitting high on a cliff.

Jennifer stared at it, stunned.

I know this house, she thought. I've looked out that second-floor window down to the cliff and the river.

It's the Conrads' house.

Trisha Conrad's house.

Jennifer turned over the parchment. A message had been scrawled on the back of the sketch. Jennifer peered at the faded handwriting.

"This drawing is given to Henry and Dominique, a gift for their new home on their wedding day, May 31, 1879. From Reverend Gabriel James, Shadyside."

Huh? I don't remember reading about Dominique getting married in the Fear Family chronicle. But she must have. It says it right here.

Jennifer stared at the sketch of the huge mansion.

Their new home, she thought.

Trisha's home.

When Dominique got married, she moved into the same house that has been in the Conrad family for generations.

Jennifer gasped.

Could Dominique Fear have married a man named Henry . . . *Conrad?*

Jennifer stared at the picture of Trisha's house. Her heart sped up, making her face flush and her hands shake.

If Dominique married a Conrad, that would mean Trisha is related to Dominique, Jennifer realized.

And *that* would mean Trisha Conrad is really a Fear!

Chapter Nineteen

"Trisha Conrad is a Fear," Jennifer said aloud.

I have to find out for sure. Jennifer dropped to the floor and frantically searched the scattered books and papers on the floor.

"Where is that chronicle?" she cried. "Where is it? Maybe I missed something!"

At last she found it. She had thrown it underneath the desk. She flipped it open on the floor and leaned over it.

Running her finger down each page, she quickly scanned the history.

"Dominique's shameful affair with Nigel Fetherston is over," Jennifer read. "But it threatened . . ."

But what about marriage? she wondered. Her

eyes poured over the page. Then she gasped.

How could I possibly have missed it? she wondered. It was right there on the page, just a few lines down.

"The family is forever indebted to Henry Conrad. For taking Dominique Fear's hand in marriage. To be willing to have her when no other man would. The date of their blessed alliance—May 31, 1879."

Jennifer sat upright. "I can't believe it," she whispered.

Dominique Fear married Henry Conrad. She used to live in the Conrad mansion.

Trisha's house.

"I can't believe it," she said again.

All those ancestors I thought were mine— they're Trisha's.

The past I thought was mine—it's Trisha's.

And she doesn't have a clue that Dominique Fear was one of her relatives. I bet none of the Conrads do. The ones that did know are probably dead now. And they probably kept it a secret.

Being descended from the Fears isn't exactly something you brag about.

It's incredible, Jennifer thought. But it makes sense. Trisha has psychic visions— just like Dominique.

And she started having the visions about Dominique and Ty when she put on that necklace.

Jennifer glanced over at the pendant. Dominique's spirit is in it. She's using it to come alive and get her revenge.

Then another thought hit her.

I need a Fear to get my revenge! That's what Trisha said when she turned into Dominique the other night.

I need a Fear.

If Dominique has to use a Fear, then maybe Trisha's the one who did all those things. Attacked Ty and set fire to his house and killed Greta. Maybe she didn't have visions about those things. Maybe she was at all those places.

Except . . .

What about my sleepwalking and my dreams? What about my glove? And almost running over Ty with my car? How come everything makes it look as if I'm the guilty one?

Could I still be involved somehow?

Jennifer shook her head, frowning. It was too complicated. She couldn't take the time to figure it out, not now anyway.

She had to do something to stop Dominique from killing again.

And she had to hurry.

She drew the book close to her and began flipping through the pages. It was like a recipe book of spells. Hundreds of them.

She found a spell to rid the house of vile

humors . . . one to stop the cows from giving sour milk . . . another that would purify the fields so the crops would grow strong . . .

Part of a sentence suddenly caught her eye. "For ridding this plane of the spirit's evil . . ."

Jennifer flattened the book and squinted at the fine print. Yes! It was a spell to send the spirit of a dead person back to the other world.

"For ridding this plane of the spirit's evil," the book instructed, "one must collect from the dead a lock of hair or a fragment of nail."

Jennifer gazed hopefully at the necklace.

"You must be certain the nail or hair truly belongs to the evil dead," the book continued. "Once you are certain, burn it until it is reduced to ashes. Thereafter, to banish the evil spirit from this plane forever, throw the ashes into the face of the person whom the spirit inhabits."

Jennifer read the whole thing a second time. Then she picked up the necklace and pulled off the garnet. She opened the compartment and stared at the coil of dark hair.

Is it Dominique's?

It might even have come from Dominique's husband, Henry. Or even her little boy.

There's no way to know for sure, Jennifer thought. I don't even know if this spell will work.

But I have to try it on Trisha right now, before something else happens.

I don't have a choice.

Carrying the lock of hair, Jennifer hurried back to the kitchen. First she tried calling Trisha's house again.

The line was busy.

She punched in Trisha's private number.

No answer.

She must be home, Jennifer thought. The answering machine isn't coming on. She's probably just not in her room.

Jennifer hung up and rummaged through the cabinets until she found a bunch of empty jars her mother had saved. She grabbed the smallest one and unscrewed the lid.

She dropped the lock of hair inside and found a box of wooden matches in the junk drawer.

The hair sizzled when the flame hit it, writhing and twisting as if it were trying to escape the fire.

In seconds all that remained was a small pile of ashes.

Jennifer shook the match out, wrinkling her nose at the smell of burned hair. She capped the jar and tried Trisha's private number again.

No answer.

She punched in the main number.

Still busy.

I can't wait, Jennifer thought. This is too important.

She grabbed her jacket and hurried outside to the car. The air felt icy, and the windshield was covered with ice and snow.

Dark gray clouds covered the sky, making it seem like evening.

Jennifer scraped the windshield, just enough so she could see, then started the car and drove toward Trisha's house.

Please let this work, she thought, glancing at the small jar of ashes on the passenger seat.

I've always hated the Fear legends. I've never believed them.

But just this once, let it work.

Chapter Twenty

Jennifer drove to the outskirts of Shadyside and way up into the hills overlooking the Conononka River. The road narrowed, and the snow from the night before forced her to slow down.

The road climbed higher, twisting and turning. On her right she saw the beginning of the high brick wall that surrounded Trisha's house and grounds.

She stopped at the iron gate and announced herself to the guards. She had to wait until her name was cleared. Hurry up, she thought impatiently. I've been here a thousand times. You know who I am.

The gate finally swung open.

Jennifer punched the pedal and guided the

car along the winding road toward the Conrad mansion.

In spring and summer the huge gardens would be full of flowers. Now, except for some holly bushes and evergreen shrubs, they seemed dull and lifeless.

The road split, one part curving toward the back of the house. Nobody ever parked in front, except for limousines. Jennifer drove to the back and parked her car on a cobblestone area near the stables.

She tucked the jar into her jacket pocket and climbed out of the car.

A wide terrace ran along the back of the house, with tall French windows leading inside. As Jennifer hurried toward the door, she could see people moving around behind the windows.

They must have company, she thought.

Of course. It's New Year's Day. I almost forgot.

Jennifer rang the bell and waited, her breath frosting in the cold air.

One of the maids answered the door. "Miss Fear," she said with a smile. "Happy New Year." She pulled the door open wide.

"Thanks. Same to you." Jennifer stepped into a foyer half the size of the main one at the front of the house. Still, it was bigger than her bedroom.

Murmuring voices and the clink of glasses

drifted from the great room at the back of the house.

The maid gestured toward Jennifer's jacket. "Shall I take that for you?"

"What? Oh. No," Jennifer told her. "Could you just get Trisha for me, please?"

"I'm sorry. She isn't here right now."

"Celia, who is it?" a woman's voice called out.

"It's Jennifer Fear, Mrs. Conrad," the maid replied.

Trisha's mother swept into the foyer, a surprised expression on her face. She had the same blond hair and delicate features as Trisha, but her eyes were a cool blue.

"Jennifer, how nice to see you!" Mrs. Conrad exclaimed. "Happy New Year."

"Thanks, Mrs. Conrad, Happy New Year. I . . . uh, I came to see Trisha," Jennifer explained, as the maid went back into the great room. "I called before and I thought she'd be back by now."

"You missed her again, I'm afraid. She came back and went out again."

"Will she be back soon?" Jennifer asked quickly.

Mrs. Conrad laughed. "Probably not. She's with Ty Sullivan—I'm sure she enjoys being with him *much* better than mingling with her father's business associates."

Jennifer stared at her in shock.

Trisha is with Ty? Jennifer felt a small pang of jealousy. Was she seeing him behind my back?

No, Jennifer reminded herself. Ty might not actually be with Trisha. He might be with *Dominique*.

Jennifer cringed as she remembered the way Dominique took over Trisha's body.

The hatred in her eyes.

The pure evil in her voice.

Dominique still wants revenge! Ty's in danger! Jennifer realized. Dominique is going to kill him! And what will Dominique do with Trisha when she's through?

"Do you know where they went?" she asked Trisha's mother.

Mrs. Conrad shook her head. "I'm afraid not. But I'll tell her to call you as soon as she gets in."

That might be too late, Jennifer thought.

She thanked Mrs. Conrad and hurried right outside to her car.

The air was bitter cold.

Jennifer started the car and flicked on the heater. Where could Ty have taken Trisha?

Maybe to Pete's. No. Pete's is closed on New Year's.

Think! Jennifer told herself. Maybe they went to the movies or someplace else to eat. Ice skating? She sighed, frustrated. They could be a hundred different places!

Then Jennifer remembered something. The special place where Ty liked to take girls.

If I know Ty, he's sure to take Trisha there. She shifted the car into gear and peeled away from Trisha's house.

I just hope I'm not too late.

Chapter Twenty-one

The road curved as the Fear Street Cemetery came into view.

The clouds grew thicker.

Darker.

It's going to snow again.

Jennifer flipped on the headlights as she drove closer to the graveyard.

Will Ty and Trisha really be here in the cemetery?

She hoped so.

Jennifer slowed down.

All she could see from the street were thick woods. The graves were on the other side of the trees.

She leaned forward, looking for the road Ty drove down that night. But she hadn't been paying attention, and she couldn't find it.

She parked the car at the side of the road and got out. Her sneakers crunched in the snow. Her breath frosted in the air, and she tucked her hands into her pockets.

Her fingers touched the smooth glass jar containing the ashes of burned hair.

Let Ty and Trisha be here.

Let the spell work, Jennifer thought.

Jennifer climbed over the crumbling stone wall and walked into the woods.

The air grew even colder.

The bare tree branches rubbed against each other in the slight breeze, making a scratching sound. Under Jennifer's feet, the fallen leaves had frozen into a solid snowy mass.

This was the last place Jennifer wanted to be, but she had to find Trisha and Ty.

She had to save them from Dominique Fear.

Fear, Jennifer thought. That's not my name.

She didn't even know her real name. She was so angry with her father that she forgot to ask.

Jennifer spotted the first gravestone.

It sat alone, chipped and sagging. Vines wrapped around it like ropes. Over the years the words carved into it had almost been erased.

Jennifer glanced around. She was still in the

woods, with no other gravestones in sight.

Why would someone be buried in such a lonely place? she wondered.

Maybe it's Dominique's, she thought, remembering what Trisha had said about them refusing to bury her in the graveyard.

She walked to the gravestone and peered at it. ALMA STR- - was all she could make out.

Not a Fear after all. She shivered and walked on.

The breeze blew again, stronger this time. The branches scratched and tapped against each other. The tree trunks swayed, making an eerie, groaning sound.

Jennifer hunched her shoulders and forced herself to keep going.

It can't be much farther, she thought. The woods will start to thin out soon. Then I'll be able to see Ty's car.

If he's here.

A clearing with three gravestones appeared on her left. The stones were black with age and grime. A few feet more and she spotted another clump of stones.

She stopped and gazed around, hoping to spot the road Ty used. Or his black Celica.

She didn't see them.

Maybe they're not here, she thought, suddenly realizing how alone she was.

Alone in a graveyard.

She took a step and froze.

What was that sound?

She held her breath and listened. A scuffling noise came from up ahead. Then a crack—like a twig snapping.

Jennifer's skin prickled.

The place gave her the creeps.

It's probably just a squirrel, she quickly told herself. Or a raccoon.

Walk a little farther, she told herself. If I don't find Ty and Trisha, I'll go home.

But if I leave, Trisha might—

No. *Dominique* might kill Ty.

Jennifer heard the scuffling noise again and forced herself to keep going.

The trees began to thin a little, and Jennifer thought she saw another clearing up ahead. She trudged through the snow toward it, nervously clutching the jar deep in her jacket pocket.

There! Through the thinning tree trunks, Jennifer spotted the rear of a black car.

Ty's Celica.

They *are* here!

She hurried forward.

A laugh suddenly rang through the woods. A wild, savage laugh that made Jennifer's skin crawl.

She froze in place, peering through the trees.

Trisha stood in the clearing.

A body lay at her feet.

Was it Ty? Jennifer couldn't tell.

Trisha raised her arm, and Jennifer caught a glimpse of something shiny and metallic. Jennifer's heart seemed to stop.

Trisha held a pair of scissors. Long and sharp.

Deadly.

Poised directly over the body's throat!

Chapter Twenty-two

"**N**ooo!" The scream burst from Jennifer's throat. "Trisha, no! Don't do it!"

Trisha stopped, the scissors poised in midair.

Jennifer held her breath, afraid to make another sound. Afraid to move.

Slowly Trisha turned her head.

Jennifer bit back another scream.

Trisha's eyes were black with fury.

Gleaming with hatred.

Jennifer could almost feel the bitterness. She had to fight the instinct to turn and run from that scalding glare.

"Trisha," she whispered. "Please. Don't."

Trisha narrowed her eyes. "I am not Trisha." Her voice was harsh and choked with rage. "My name is Dominique."

Dominique. That's why Trisha looks so wild, Jennifer realized. Dominique has totally possessed her.

And Trisha's not even wearing the necklace.

When she first put it on, she just had a vision. The second time she *became* Dominique.

Somehow, Dominique's spirit doesn't need the necklace anymore.

What am I going to do? Jennifer wondered. How am I going to stop this?

Jennifer took a cautious step forward. "Uh, Dominique?" she murmured. "Please put the scissors down." She took another step.

Trisha's body tensed. Her hand tightened around the gleaming weapon.

Jennifer halted, her heart pounding. She glanced at the body on the ground.

It *was* Ty.

He lay on his back, his head turned slightly to the side. Leaves clung to his face. His blond hair was wet with melted snow. Mud smeared his cheeks and lips.

His jacket had fallen open, exposing his blue sweater.

And his bare throat.

His eyes were closed.

Is he breathing? Jennifer wondered frantically. I can't tell. But I don't see any blood.

Maybe he fell and hit his head or something.

Jennifer raised her eyes and met Trisha's angry gaze.

"You can't let Dominique do this, Trish," Jennifer said slowly. "You can fight her. I know you can!"

Trisha threw back her long blond hair and laughed viciously. "Trisha is no longer with us."

"No!" Jennifer cried, taking several steps forward. "Trisha, snap out of it. Fight her!"

Trisha lurched toward Jennifer, jabbing the sharp scissors. "Do not come closer!" she wailed.

Jennifer gasped, and stepped back.

Trisha whirled around to face Ty. She grabbed the scissors with both hands and slowly raised them above her head.

She's going to kill Ty, Jennifer realized. Right here in front of me. I have to stop it!

"I know why you're here, uh, *Dominique,*" Jennifer blurted out. "But killing Ty won't change anything. It won't bring Nigel back."

Trisha turned her head. Her lips twisted. "What do you know of Nigel?"

"I know you loved him," Jennifer told her. "You thought he loved you, but he didn't."

Trisha's eyes flashed. "He betrayed me! And then he cast me aside."

"I know," Jennifer said softly. "Then you were hanged for killing him. But you didn't

133

do it. And you want revenge."

"Yes!" Trisha laughed again, an ugly, bitter sound. "And I will have it!"

Jennifer pointed to Ty. "Not by killing *him*."

"True. Not him alone," Trisha agreed. "First I had to kill the one he deserted me for. And I did that."

Greta, Jennifer realized. Greta was going with Ty, so Trisha killed her.

No, not Trisha, she reminded herself. Dominique.

"And now it is Nigel's turn."

"But that's *not* Nigel," Jennifer tried to reason with Dominique. "What good will killing *Ty* do? It won't get you revenge."

Trisha smiled slyly. "But no one will know *I* did it. Everyone will think it was *you!*"

Jennifer gasped.

"People already think you murdered that woman Nigel left me for." Trisha laughed. "I saw to that. I pulled that shelf down so the bowl would fall on her head. Crack!"

Jennifer jumped. Her heart pounded harder in her chest.

"Her skull splintered like dry wood!" Trisha declared triumphantly. "Nigel thinks you did it. He said so. And when he dies, people will suspect you. After all, you attacked him in his yard. You set fire to his house.

134

"No!" Jennifer cried. "You made Trisha do it! I wasn't even there!"

"Oh, but you were." Trisha lowered the gleaming scissors and smiled. "Do you not remember your *dreams?* How you searched for him? How you lit the match?"

Jennifer shivered. "That was me? But—"

"No," Trisha said. "That was not you. Only a *true* Fear can help me complete my purpose!"

Jennifer let out her breath in relief.

"You were a witness," Trisha went on. "But the town will think you are a killer. They will think you did everything. And you left your glove behind to prove it!"

She wants me to be accused of murder! Jennifer thought. "Why?" she whispered shakily.

"So you will know what it is really like to be a Fear!" Trisha shouted. "To be wrongly accused!"

"But I'm *not* a Fear!" Jennifer cried out.

"I know." Trisha seethed. "You are a liar. Just as those who hanged me were liars. And you shall pay!"

Trisha flung her hair back and tightened her grip on the scissors. "But first it is Nigel's turn," she muttered.

"Trisha, please!" Jennifer screamed. "You can't let Dominique do this!" Without thinking, Jennifer rushed toward Trisha.

"No!" Trisha screamed. "You cannot stop me! No one can stop me. I will have my revenge!"

With a roar of fury Trisha lunged toward Jennifer.

The scissor blades flashed.

Jennifer screamed and leaped aside.

Trisha stopped herself from falling and whirled around. The blades flashed again as she swung the scissors toward Jennifer's face.

Jennifer dodged away, screaming again.

As Trisha plunged forward, Jennifer shoved her from the side.

Trisha stumbled but did not fall. She gained her balance and quickly rushed toward Ty.

"Nooo!" Jennifer ran after her and started to push her again.

Trisha spun quickly. The scissors slashed the air.

Jennifer felt a sharp, stinging pain in her right hand. She cried out, grasping her wrist. A line of bright red blood oozed across her palm.

Trisha's wild laugh rang through the graveyard again.

Panting with terror, Jennifer raced around Ty's body. She's going to kill me! she thought.

Dominique is going to kill me!

Jennifer glanced around, frantically scanning the clearing for some sort of weapon. A branch. A rock. Anything.

Then she remembered.

The ashes!

Use the ashes, she told herself. Throw them in her face.

It was her only chance.

Trisha stepped over Ty's body.

Jennifer stumbled backward and banged up against a tree at the edge of the clearing.

Trisha laughed. She tossed her hair from her eyes and tightened her grip on the scissors.

Jennifer slid her hand into her pocket and pulled out the jar.

Blood covered her palm now. The jar grew slippery with it and almost fell out of her grasp.

Trisha stalked toward Jennifer.

Jennifer wiped her bloody hand on her jeans and tried to unscrew the lid. The blood kept seeping out. The jar grew slick again.

Trisha came closer, crunching the snow under her shoes.

Whimpering in fear, Jennifer twisted the lid again.

It opened with a small snap. Gasping in relief, Jennifer unscrewed it and dropped it to the ground.

"Is that your weapon?" Trisha asked with a laugh in her voice.

Jennifer gripped the jar as tightly as she could. Her knees felt weak. Too weak to hold her up.

She braced herself against the tree and waited for Trisha to come closer.

Please let it work, she prayed. Let the ashes be from Dominique's hair.

The snow crunched again as Trisha moved even closer.

I can't miss, Jennifer told herself desperately. I'll only have this one chance!

Her hand shook. She couldn't steady it.

But there was no more time.

Trisha quickly stepped forward and raised the knife.

Jennifer gripped the jar by the bottom and swung it underhanded.

The ashes flew out in a dark puff, straight into Trisha's face.

Chapter Twenty-three

"**A**aaahh!" Trisha let out a wailing howl of agony and dropped the scissors.

"My eyes!" she shrieked, clawing at her face. She grabbed a handful of snow and rubbed it on her eyes. "They're on fire! My eyes are burning!"

Trisha screamed again. She dug her knuckles into her eyes, desperately trying to get the ashes out.

Jennifer watched, shaken and terrified.

The spell book never said anything like this would happen, she thought.

What did I do to her?

Will Trisha be blind?

Will she still be Dominique?

Trisha let out a final scream, then dropped to her knees.

She hung her head and braced her hands in the dirt. Her shoulders began to shake. A sob burst from her throat, and she collapsed to the ground, crying and trembling.

Jennifer waited, eyeing her cautiously. Is she still Dominique, or is the evil spirit gone?

Be ready to run, she told herself.

Trisha's sobs gradually faded. She shifted on the ground and slowly raised her head.

Jennifer's muscles tensed.

Trisha brushed her hair away with a shaky hand. Her face was sooty with ashes and streaked with tears.

She looked confused.

"Trisha?" Jennifer whispered.

Trisha blinked and glanced up. "Jen?"

"Thank goodness!" Jennifer cried. She pushed herself away from the tree and ran to Trisha's side.

"What am I doing here?" Trisha asked shakily.

Trisha doesn't remember, Jennifer thought. She doesn't have a clue what's happened.

As Trisha pushed herself to her knees, she noticed the bloody scissors lying in the dirt. "Jen, look!"

"I know." Jennifer took Trisha's arm and helped her to her feet. "You didn't hurt me. Well, just my hand, but it's okay. Don't worry."

"What do you mean? Are those *mine*?"

Jennifer nodded.

"But what . . ." Trisha gazed around the clearing and spotted Ty. "What is he doing here?"

"He . . . you came here with him," Jennifer told her.

Trisha shook her head in confusion. "I don't understand. And why is he lying there like that? What happened to him?"

Without meaning to, Jennifer glanced at the scissors.

Trisha followed her gaze. "Oh, no!" she cried. "Is he dead? Did I kill Ty? I'm a murderer! I must have killed Greta, too!"

"No! *You* didn't kill anybody," Jennifer told her. "It was Dominique."

"Huh?"

Has she blocked it out? Jennifer wondered. "Dominique Fear," she said. "You remember the necklace I got for Christmas, don't you? Dominique's name is on it. And . . . her spirit was *in* it."

"Oh. Yes. Now I remember." Trisha rubbed her eyes. "But what does Dominique have to do with me?"

I can't tell her now, Jennifer thought. It'll be too much of a shock. "It's a long story," she replied. "You won't believe it. *I* still can't believe it."

"But . . ."

A soft groan drifted through the clearing.

Jennifer whipped her head around and stared at Ty.

His legs shifted slightly and his eyebrows twitched. He groaned again.

"He's alive!" Jennifer cried out. "Thank goodness, he's alive!"

"But I still don't understand why we came here," Trisha said.

"This is the place he likes to take girls. To make out with them." Jennifer hesitated. "Trisha . . . were you seeing Ty behind my back?"

"What?" Trisha's eyes widened in surprise. "No! I don't even know what happened."

Jennifer smiled. *I knew Trisha wouldn't betray me like that,* she thought.

"Jen, tell me what's going on," Trisha pleaded.

Ty groaned again, louder this time. His head moved from side to side and his eyelids fluttered.

Jennifer gasped. "Quick. We have to get him out of here before he wakes up, or he'll think I tried to kill him again. No way will I ever be able to explain it."

"I wish you'd explain it to me," Trisha declared.

"I will. I promise," Jennifer told her. "Let's just get him out of here first."

Ty moaned, rolling his head back and forth.

"Hurry, Trisha!" Jennifer cried. "Help me get him into his car. We'll take him home and come up with a story later. Okay?"

Trisha gave her a weak smile. "Okay."

Chapter Twenty-four

Jennifer lifted her slice of pizza and prepared to take a bite.

"That looks totally disgusting," Trisha remarked.

Jennifer paused. "What does?"

"Pineapple and pepperoni."

"It's great," Jennifer declared. "Want to try it?"

Trisha shuddered. "No, thanks. I'll stick to plain cheese."

Jennifer laughed and bit into her pizza. The perfect combination, she decided as she chewed.

She swallowed and sipped some Coke, glancing around Pete's Pizza.

The place was crowded. School started tomorrow, and everybody seemed to want to hang out one last time.

Josie Maxwell rushed from table to table, taking orders and delivering pizza and burgers.

Josie's stepbrother, Josh, sat with Kenny Klein and Jade Feldman.

Matty Winger stood at Mickey Myer's table, telling jokes and obviously bothering Mickey's girlfriend, Dana Palmer.

Everything seems so normal, Jennifer told herself. It's like nothing bad ever happened in Shadyside.

She took another bite of pizza. And only two days ago Trisha and I were fighting in the cemetery, she thought. Now *we're* back to normal, too. "Where's Gary?" she asked.

Trisha glanced up from the fashion magazine she'd been looking at. "He's working on his car. It's such a total waste of time."

Jennifer nodded. But what is Gary supposed to do? she wondered. He and his mother can barely afford to pay the rent on their house in Shadyside's poor section of town. He can't exactly afford a new car.

Jennifer started to drink some more Coke and stopped with the glass halfway to her mouth. The tiny bell to the door jingled.

"Oh, no," she murmured. "Ty just came in. And he's heading our way."

"Do you think he remembers anything?" Trisha whispered anxiously.

"I don't know. I guess we're going to find

out." Jennifer lowered her glass and waited as Ty edged his way around some tables.

He still wore a bandage on the side of his forehead, but it was smaller. No ugly stitches poked out from the sides.

Ty stopped at the booth. "Hi, Trisha."

Trisha closed the magazine and smiled nervously. "Hi."

A faint flush rose up his neck and spread across his cheeks. "I . . . uh . . . I want to apologize for the other night," he told her. "I acted like a major jerk, getting drunk like that."

Jennifer looked away so Ty wouldn't see the expression of relief on her face.

He believed our story, she thought. He thinks he took Trisha to the cemetery, drank too much beer, and passed out. That she called me on her cell phone and I helped her get him home.

"I still can't believe I passed out on you," Ty went on. "I don't even remember drinking. But anyway, no excuses. I'm sorry."

"It's okay," Trisha told him. "Don't worry about it."

"Thanks." Ty brushed a hand over his hair and turned to Jennifer. "And, uh, thanks for helping her take me home," he added. "Especially after, you know, everything."

Jennifer stared at him, surprised he was even speaking to her. "Sure."

146

"Um . . ." Ty hesitated. "The police talked to me yesterday," he declared. "They're positive Greta died accidentally. They explained the whole thing to me and I believe them. I owe you an apology, too, Jennifer. For accusing you."

Jennifer managed a smile. "Thanks."

What else can I say? she wondered. That the police are wrong? Except I didn't kill Greta, Dominique Fear did?

"Okay. So . . . see you back at school." Ty gave them both an embarrassed smile and quickly walked away.

Jennifer glanced at Trisha.

"That's great, isn't it?" Trisha said. "It's actually over, and nobody knows what happened. Nobody would believe it, anyway, right?"

"Right," Jennifer agreed.

Trisha slid out of the booth. "I have to use the bathroom. Be back in a minute."

Jennifer picked up her pizza and took another bite. It *is* over, she told herself.

Dominique's evil spirit is gone.

Jennifer pictured the necklace in her mind. She had put it in a box and stuffed the box in the back of her closet.

Dominique doesn't control it anymore, she thought. She can never make someone kill again. When I burned the hair and threw it in Trisha's face, I killed Dominique's spirit for good.

And I'm not a Fear. That's the best news. For me, anyway.

Jennifer sighed. What about Trisha? she wondered. Her friend didn't seem to care that she was a Fear. But Jennifer couldn't help worrying.

What will happen to Trisha now that she knows the truth?

Chapter Twenty-five

Trisha slid back into the booth and quickly took a bite of her pizza.

Cold.

She forced herself to chew anyway. She didn't want to talk yet. She might sound too nervous, and Jen would notice immediately.

Trisha opened the magazine and gazed at a picture without really seeing it. She swallowed and cleared her throat. "So. Are you talking to your father yet?" she asked, not raising her eyes.

"Barely," Jennifer replied. "I haven't even asked him what our real name is. And I'll never respect him again, that's for sure. What a liar."

Good, Trisha thought. She hasn't told him

about me. "And we're still going to keep everything a secret, right?"

"Definitely," Jennifer assured her.

Trisha felt a flood of relief. No one but Jennifer knows I'm a Fear.

And she won't tell anybody.

Trisha tightened her lips. *She'd better not.*

"My turn," Jennifer said. She scooted out of the booth and went into the bathroom.

Trisha gazed after her. Jen's such a good friend, she thought. I still can't believe I went out with Ty behind her back. Not just once or twice, either.

Dozens of times.

And at the graveyard—I *was* making out with him. Then . . . everything went black. The next thing I saw was Jennifer's face.

She was terrified. Of me!

Trisha reached for her soda, but her hand was shaking. She grabbed a napkin instead.

She needed something to hold on to.

It was so confusing at first, she thought. But once I realized what Dominique wanted, everything was easy.

It was easy because I'm a Fear.

Trisha closed her fist over the napkin, squeezing it into a tight ball.

At the moment she felt terrified. Helpless.

But sometimes she felt an intense rage slowly burning inside her. She just couldn't control it. The rage burned hotter and faster until she wanted to scream. To strike out.

To kill.

I have to be careful, she thought. I have to control myself. I don't want to be like all the other Fears.

She squeezed her fist even tighter.

Dominique is dead, she reminded herself.

The evil is gone. Jennifer threw the ashes in my face.

She got rid of it!

Trisha's knuckles turned white.

I hope.

R.L. Stine
Seniors
a FEAR STREET series

available from Gold Key® Paperbacks

FEAR STREET® Sagas

FEAR STREET® titles

About R.L. Stine

R.L. Stine is the best-selling author in America. He has written more than one hundred scary books for young people, all of them bestsellers.

His series include *Fear Street, Fear Street Seniors,* and the *Fear Street Sagas.*

Bob grew up in Columbus, Ohio. Today he lives in New York City with his wife, Jane, his son, Matt, and his dog, Nadine.

Do you know the address for Fear?

www.fearstreet.com

Connect to the curse of **The Fear Family** with the brand new **Fear Street Website!** This scary site brings you up close and personal with the legend of the Fears and their legacy of blood. With sneak peeks of upcoming stories, top secret information, games, gossip, and the latest buzz on who will survive from the brain of R.L Stine, this is your chance to know the deadly truth.

Get caught in the web of fear!

Don't Miss **FEAR STREET®** Seniors
Episode Seven!

FIGHT, TEAM, FIGHT!

Phoebe Yamura loves being a cheerleader.

And her senior year at Shadyside High couldn't be more perfect. First she's voted captain of the squad. And now she's seeing Ty Sullivan.

But if Phoebe is so perfect, why does somebody want her dead?